Demons Destiny

Kayla Pickett

Contents

Chapter One

T rigger Warning: There is an attempted sexual assault scene in this chapter. If this triggers anyone, please skip.

Standing on the ladder, I carefully place the bright yellow star on top of the Christmas tree. I smile, admiring my work. Leah's going to freak when she open's up tomorrow morning. My coworker, Chris, and I knew she was devastated that she wasn't able to afford one for the shop this year so we decided to pitch in and surprise her."You done up there?" I jump at the sudden sound and lose my footing. I yelp as I start to fall to the ground but Chris's arms are around me, breaking my fall. Still, my ankle throbs. I must have twisted it on my way down."Shit! I'm sorry, I didn't mean to sneak up on you like that, Sephie," He says. My cheeks burn and I know embarrassment isn't the only reason why. Chris's arms feel quite good around me and I can smell his cologne from this close."It's fine, I should have been paying attention. I'm such a clutz," Chris steadies me and lets me go. I wince as my ankle throbs from all the weight on it."You need to get some ice on that when you get home. And I hope you know there's no way I'm letting you walk home in that condition.""The bus stop is just down the street. It's no big deal," I say, desperately hoping he takes my word for it. I can't let him see the neighborhood I live in. He wouldn't think of me the same again."Not happening.""My ankle doesn't even hurt that bad. See," I say, lifting my leg and twirling my foot around to convince him. I try to smile through clenched teeth as the throbbing pain intensifies. "The bus drops me off close to my house. I'll only be walking for ten minutes at most.""Are you sure," He asks, looking doubtful."Yep. I'll be fine. I promise," I assure him, trying to look as convincing as possible."Okay, but be careful. I'll see you tomorrow."Chris and I lock up before leaving. It's just past seven and the sun is beginning to set. I wave at Chris as we go in opposite directions. As soon as I turn the corner and am out of the eyesight of Chris I limp, the pressure on my ankle too painful. I wasn't lying when I said the bus stop was close but it drops me off twenty minutes from my house.I wear my earbuds on the bus, gazing out the window as the bus travels through town. One of my hobbies is people watching and I do it every day on my way home. I smile, looking as a woman kneels in front of her upset son and puts a bandaid on his knee. Afterward, she places a kiss on his boo-boo and helps him up. It's cute but it leaves me feeling bitter. I wish I had a loving mother like that. My mother is probably passed out on the couch at this moment, beer bottle in hand. That's usually the scene I come home to when I get off of work.I still wear my earbuds as I get off the bus. Even though my ankle is still sore I try to speed up my pace. I live on the bad side of town and It's not the safest place to walk alone. I just keep my head down and try not to draw attention to myself. By the time I reach the trailer park my ankle is absolutely throbbing. I fumble with my keys, desperate to ice it. I hurry inside and immediately go to the freezer and take out an icepack."Mom! I'm home," I call out, even though I know she's probably passed out."She's not here," For the second time today I jump in fear and the ice pack tumbles out of hand and falls to the floor. I turn around and there's a strange man standing in my living room. He looks dangerous, almost six feet tall with a bald head and tattoos down his neck and some on his face."Who are you? Get out of my house or I'm calling the police," I try to sound assertive but voice trembles. There are only about fifteen feet between us and it wouldn't take long for him to cross the distance."We both know that's not happening," He says in a cool voice that sends chills down my spine. "Now why don't you have a seat."He starts to walk towards me and I grab the nearest thing to me and weald it as a weapon. To my dismay, It's a measly pair of tongs. Before I know it, he snatches them from my hand and they fly across the room and hit the wall. He painfully grips my arm and drags me into the living room and throws me onto the couch."That's your first lesson. You can cooperate or I can make you cooperate.""Please don't h-hurt me. Just leave, I won't call the police or anything if you just leave now," Tears fall down my cheeks and I'm terrified. There not much I can do to defend myself and this guy could kill me right now if he really wanted to."You're not calling the police either way. Now, we have things to discuss. Three days ago your mother stole from me and my club. You can imagine that I'm very pissed right now." I knew my mother had something to do with this. She has a gambling addiction and a drinking habit and she's been low on money these past few months. Still, I didn't think she would go as far as putting us in danger for money."If you want money you can have it. Just take whatever you want and leave me alone.""Trust me, you don't have nearly enough to pay me off. Lisa stole fifty thousand dollars from my club," My jaw nearly falls into my lap. After the shock subsides rage fills me. She can pull some grand heist but she can't get a job? I've been working day and night to pay the bills around here and she pulls this and leaves me to face the replications."She's already skipped town. Since she can't pay her debt, you'll do it for her. Since I doubt you got fifty thousand lying around, you'll be doing it with your body," My blood runs cold as ice. I think about getting up and running towards the door, but I know he'll catch me."My dad's a lawyer! I'll call him up and he'll pay you," That's complete baloney but I hope he buys it. My dad was a janitor and he skipped town when I was six."If your dad was a lawyer, you wouldn't be livin' in a trailer. Now, before I sell you, I want to have a taste. Soon you're be all used up," I scream as he gets on top of me but he covers my mouth with his hand. I bite his palm as hard as I can and metallic blood fills my mouth."Fuckin bitch!" He snarls. His fist crashes against my cheek and burning pain scorches the side of my face. I fight as hard as I can but it doesn't have any effect on him. He pulls the neck of the sweater I'm wearing the buttons pop off and my bra is revealed. Panicking, I reach around for something I can defend myself with. Behind me, my fingers touch cold porcelain. I grab the vase and smash on top of his head as hard as I can. It breaks into pieces all over us and he falls limp on top of me, sobs wracking my body. He begins to stir on top of me which sends me into action. I push him off of me and get up, the broken pieces of the vase falling to the floor. I race out the front door and run as fast as I can. People stare at me and I don't blame them. My sweater is completely ripped in the front but I can't bring myself to be embarrassed at the indecency. I make many turns so it'll be hard for him to find me when he regains consciousness. Soon the burning in my legs overpowers the fear and adrenaline so I have to stop running. I get out my phone but it's powered off. Luckily, there is a payphone near me. I only have enough for two calls. When I pick up the phone my fingers hover over the keys and I realize that I don't know who to call. I don't know Chris's number and the police aren't an option. I don't think I can handle being questioned and reliving what happened and filing police reports. Plus, if they don't catch him there's no doubt he will come after me for snitching.There is really only one person I can think of. I punch in their number and anxiously wait as the call goes through. It goes to voicemail so I put in the last bit of change I have left and hope. Please, please go through, I pray."Hello," Her groggy voice answers. Relief fills me and tears fall down my cheeks at the sound of her voice

Chapter Two

Mia's PovThe annoyingly loud sound of my phone ringing pierces through my dream world. I mentally curse those goddamn telemarketers. They've been blowing me up ever since I got my new phone. I'm relieved when the sound stops and I began to drift off again. The phone rings again and I want to throw it across the room."Answer the phone, Mia," Silas mumbles beside me. I know he's right, it must be someone important if they called twice. Still, I want to kick him in the shin. I reach over to grab my phone from its charger but it slips from my finger onto the floor. Annoyed, I fumble for it on the side of the bed in the dark. It's too late for this shit."Hello," I groggily say into the phone just before it's about to stop ringing. I swear to god, if this isn't an emergency whoever this is is going to get an earful."I really need your help, Mia," My heart drops to the pit of my stomach and I'm immediately wide awake. My sister's voice trembles so I know something's happened."Oh my god, Sephie! What's wrong?" My panicked voice alerts Silas and he's up too, his worried eyes questioning me."Mom stole a bunch of money from some people and now they want to hurt me. I really need you to come get me," Silas overhears what she said and he's up, throwing on his clothes and putting his shoes on."Where are you? I'm leaving now," I get out of bed and slide on my shoes and robe as Sephie tells me the address."I need you to stay on the phone with me, okay? I'm walking out the door right now," Silas is already in the car, waiting for me when I get in."The calls going to end soon and I don't have enough money to make another one,""Shit! Well just wait right there. We're driving as fast as we can,""Okay. Be careful." I assure I will but neither Silas or I are very concerned with the road safety laws at the moment. The call ends and my anxiety is back. I have no way of knowing if she's safe or not. For all I know, she can be in the back of some thug's car right now."I'm going to kill my mom," I inform Silas. It's just like her to put her children in danger to support her little addiction. I vow to myself to ring her neck next time I see her."I would advise you not to but I won't stop you.""I can't believe her! She cares more about drugs and gambling than her kids. I shouldn't have let my sister stay there. I knew-""This isn't your fault," He reaches over and comfortingly squeezes my knee. "There is no way you could have saw this coming." His words ease my guilt but anxiety still hangs over me like a dark cloud.The address Sephie gave is all the way on the other side of town but Silas is driving like a bat from hell. I pray we don't get pulled over as he breaks tons of laws. As we approach the address and I look outside for any sign of my sister. I spot her curly-headed figure standing by a payphone, arms wrapped around herself."There she is!" I tell Silas. I jump out of the car before he's even come to a full stop. As soon as I get to my sister, I pull her into my arms."I was so worried, Sephie." "Me too," I hold her at arm's length and examine. Her right eye and cheekbone are completely bruised and the button up sweater she wearing is ripped open."Did he...uh- hurt you." Rage bubbles up in me and I want to hunt whoever did this down and kick their ass."He tried to but I'm okay, Mia, I promise," She tries to assure me but I know her too well."You absolutely are not and that's okay. You have every right to be upset right now," Tears well up her eyes and I take her into my arms again.When Sephie is done crying Silas opens the car door for her to get in. Silas still speeds but he's more careful now. Sephie is already a wreck and we don't need to get pulled over. The atmosphere in the car is tense and I can feel Silas seething beside me. Silas doesn't take kindly to people hurting the people he cares about.

Even though he's never met Sephie he knows I love her so she falls onto that list.When we arrive at the house, Silas helps Sephie out of the car and I notice she walks with a limp. "We have an extra room but you'll have to use the hallway bathroom. I have some extra clothes you can borrow. I'll go get you an ice pack so you can get settled in," I show Sephie to her room and hand her the ice pack. I quickly go to the room Silas and I share and I look through our dresser for clothes she can borrow. She a couple sizes larger than I am so I gather all the things that are oversized on me. When I go to the room she's sitting on the bed, staring out the window."I'll leave you alone but I want you to know Silas and I are going to handle this," I tell her, stetting the pile of folded clothes on her bed."I know. Thank you," Her voice is quiet and I know she must be traumatized right now and needs some space. I leave her be and go back up to our room and Silas is sitting on the bed, on the phone."...My girlfriend's little sister's just been attacked so I'm not in the best mood right now. I need a guy here, ASAP," He pauses as the person on the other line talks. "Okay. I'll see you.""What was that about?" I ask but I think I already know. Silas used to be an underground fighter and knows a lot of people who dabble in things outside the law. He's gotten out of that life now and owns a business now but he's still known for his fighting days."A buddy of mine is coming over tomorrow. We're going to find the guy who did this and make him pay. We're also going to find your mom and make her give the money back," The way Silas says it I know there is no arguing. He's always protecting the people in his circle and I love him for it."Thank you, Honey," I stand in between his legs and take his face in my hands and place a soft kiss on his lips. For the moment, I feel like everything is going to be alright.

Turn that little star orange for some good luck!

Chapter Three

- -

S ephie POV

I notice the throbbing pain in my eye and cheekbone as soon as I wake up. When I open my eyes I'm confused for a second by the unfamiliar room, them I remember the events of yesterday. Suddenly, I don't want to get up and face the world. Soon, my bladder overcomes my desire to hide from the world and I'm forced to get up.

When I stare in the mirror for the first time, I wince. Varying shades of purple, blue, and green paint my eye and cheekbone. My curly hair in a mess on my head. In the stress of yesterday, I forgot to tie it up last night. Overall, I look like a wreck, which is pretty accurate considering how I feel.

After doing my business, I try to tame my hair but give up and end up putting it in a messy bun. I leave the bathroom looking like a more re-freshed wreck.

"Sephie," I hear my sister call. I follow her voice into the kitchen. We didn't talk much yesterday and I know she has a lot to say to me. We talk every day on the phone but we haven't seen each other in person since she moved out three years ago. Between me working and her going to beauty school, we've grown apart.

"How'd you sleep?" She asks.

"Like the dead," I sit at the counter and admire the house. I know it must be her boyfriends because of how masculine and modern it looks. From what she's told me during our phone conversations, she recently moved in with him. I know once she gets a chance to decorate it will look much homier.

"That's good," She sits a bowl in front of me and pours my favorite cereal in, the one with the little cookies. I want to tell I can do it myself but I know she won't listen. She always took on the maternal role in our sisterhood. Our mother's neglectfulness made it worse and I know she feels responsible for me.

"Silas is outside talking to some people. They're probably going to ask you some questions about last night."

"Are they cops?" I ask, dreading it. I just want to forget about what happened and the whole legal process just seems draining.

"No, far from it. They're friends of Silas and they are going to help us."

"Oh my god, please don't tell me you're dating a drug dealer," I say, rolling my eyes. Her boyfriend did look a little rough, dark brown hair, lean muscles, and I noticed a sleeve of tattoos.

"No, and you shouldn't be so quick to judge," She scolds me, sending me a look over her shoulder as she takes a jug of milk out of the fridge. "He used to be an underground boxer but now he owns his own business. He knows a few people who can track our mom down and find the people who did this."

"Oh, well that's a relief! He's just an ex illegal fighter with dangerous criminal friends. I'm not surprised, you've always been into the bad boys. Remember Blake?" I say, referencing her highschool boyfriend.

"Blake is a part of my past I'd like to forget. You know I wouldn't let you around Silas if I didn't trust he was a danger," She pours the milk into my bowl as she talks.

"Okay, I'll give the guy a chance. I can see why you like him, he's hot," Mia gets a dreamy look on her face but before she can gross me out with her lovey-dovey talk, the front door opens and three men walk. I thought Silas looked rough but these guys are total units. One has to be over 6'2 with blond hair and a jagged scar that runs down the left side of his face. The other is even taller, with inky black hair that needs a cut and a face that could have been carved by Michelangelo himself. Tattoos peek from the neckline of his shirt and I'm sure he's covered in them.

"This is Ace and Demon." Silas introduced them. The blond one, Ace, tilts his chin up at me but Demon's eyes get hard and I notice the muscles in his jaw tighten. "They're going to ask you a few questions about last night."

Ace takes a seat next to me but Demon remains standing, still looking pissed off. I can't help but think the name fits him.

"We need to know everything that happened, from the moment you arrived home yesterday," Ace informs me.

"Uh- well, when I got home from work I noticed him in my house."

"Did you see a car in the driveway?" Ace asks.

"No, I wasn't really paying attention," I admit, feeling like an idiot. "He grabbed my arm and dragged me over to the couch. He told me my mom stole 50,000 from 'him and his club'. He said that since they couldn't find her he was going to make me pay her debt...with my body."

Demon's eyes get hard again and even Ace looks angry. I realize that Demon didn't look angry because he didn't like me, but because of the black eye I'm sporting. The thought sends a strangely soft feeling through me.

"Did he say what club?"

"No, he didn't mention it. After that, he tried to assault me. We struggled for a while and I hit him over the head with a vase. After that, I ran out of there and called Mia," I finish.

"I think it was the local MC. They're always causing trouble around here," Ace says.

"Our mom was seeing someone there. I think his name was Mark or something. She must have gotten the money through him," I tell him.

"She's not too smart. She's definitely blowing a ton of money. We'll follow the crash trail right to her," Silas says. "In the meantime, you don't go anywhere by yourself. If you have places to go, I'll take you. If I'm not available then Demon will take you."

With that, Demon and Ace leave. I finish eating my now soggy cereal and call my job to let them know why I'm gone.

"This is Leah's Bookshop, how can I help you," Chris answers. Even his voice sends flutters in my belly.

"This is Sephie," I wince, waiting for him to freak out.

"We were supposed to surprise Leah today! I had to do it all by myself," Chris exclaims.

"Someone broke into my house yesterday and assaulted me. I'm at my sister's place right now."

"Oh my god! Are you okay? I should have never let you go home alone, this is all my fault."

"That's not true. I'm the one who convinced you to let me go alone," I say, feeling bad that he feels guilty because of me.

"Listen, a customer just came in but I'm going to call you back at the end of my shift. Take the week off, you need to recover. And I'm never letting you go home alone ever again. Take care of yourself, Sephie."

"I will, Chris. Talk to you later."

"Was that your boyfriend?" I jump, almost dropping the phone. She must have been listening to my whole conversation.

"No, he's just this guy I work with," I say, hoping she doesn't press the issue.

"You like him don't you?" She says with a Cheshire Cat grin. My first instinct is to lie, but I think it will be a relief to finally have someone to gush about him to.

"Yeah, I do. We used to go to school with him, he's Christopher Hale."

"Oh, he's cute! Tell me all about him!"

Mia and sit at the counter and I tell her all about how my heart flutters when he's near and she listens with avid, dreamy eyes. For a little while, I forget about the mess I'm in.

Turn that little star orange for some good luck!

Chapter Four

Demon's POVThe sickening thud of fist hitting flesh sounds off. Jake falls to the concrete ground along with two of his teeth. He's completely still on the ground and like always I check to make sure he's breathing. The crowd is going crazy and their chants of my name are dea fening."Demon has done it again! Another KO in less than a minute. He still has yet to be defeated!" The balding man screams into the megaphone. The crowd goes crazy once again and I try to make my way out of there without starting a riot. Some of my guys have to hold them back so we can leave.Later on in the night, I watch as the people around me drink from red solo cups and grind against each other. This is my celebration party, though it seems like I'm the only one not having fun. A slender blonde eyes me from across the room but I ignore her. Honestly, I'm tired of all the meaningless hookups. They used to be exciting but now they're all the same."You got a minute, Demon?" Ace says, approaching me."Sure," I answer."Silas just called. His girlfriend's sister got attacked and he's pretty pissed about it," My lips tighten. Silas is a long-time friend of mine and if he's got a problem I got a problem. And I'm not too fond of women getting attacked."They know who did it?""Nope. Apparently her mom stole money from some bad people.""We goin' now?" I ask, ready to find whoever did this and show them how I got my name."The girl's pretty shaken up right now. It's best if we go in the morning.""I'll be there," I say. Ace goes back to the chick he was talking to and I decide to ditch my own party. The blonde gives me a seductive smile as I pass her but I continue to ignore her.***Silas is standing outside when we approach the house. He wastes no time, getting right into it as soon as we're out of the car."Sephie didn't tell us much yesterday, she was pretty banged up. All we know right now is that her mother stole money, skipped town, and left her to pay the repercussions."We'll ask her some questions and go lookin' for her mother and that asshole," Ace says."Okay, but be gentle on her. She's been through a lot," He warns. I spot her as soon as I walk in, sitting at the counter next to Silas's girl. I only see her side profile from this angle. She looks like her sister, except a lot curvier. Her curly hair is in a bun at the top of her hair and she's wearing a pair of grey sweats and a t-shirt."This is Ace and Demon. They're going to ask you a few questions about last night." Silas introduces us. Sephie turns around to face us and I notice her blackened eye. It startles me to see such a beautiful face banged up. The girl doesn't look like she could hurt a fly and yet some asshole tried to hurt her. I think of all the ways I'm going to kick this guy's ass when I get my hands on him.She goes into her story and Ace asks her questions. When she gets to the part about him threatening to sell her body, fury burns through my veins as I'm sure it does Silas and Ace. Even Mia looks like she wants to kick someone's ass. Ace, Silas and I leave when she's done."We gotta find this asshole," I say as soon we're out of earshot. I kept quiet while we were in there because I knew in that moment, anything that came out of my mouth would terrify the girl."I'm already on it," Ace says. "Her mom's got a gambling problem. No way she not blowing through that money like crazy. I'll check with all the casinos around here for big spenders.""She's gonna need someone with her everywhere she goes from now on. I'm busy with my business so I'm unavailable a lot," Silas says."I'll do it," I volunteer. Ace's wife is pregnant and about ready to pop any day now so I know he wants to be around her. I also can't deny the fact that I want to be the one protecting her."Thank you. I owe you for this," Silas says. Ace and I take off. The whole ride I think about Sephie and her curly hair and curvy figure.

Turn that little star orange for some good luck!

Chapter Five

S ephie POV

ONE WEEK LATERI wake up excited that I finally get to go to work again. This past week has been pretty boring. Mia and I always have to have Silas or Demon with us when we go out and since Silas is busy it's been Demon more often. The only time we really went out was when Mia took me to the mall to buy clothes, which I protested, but we all know there's no talking Mia out of anything. Mia and I spent most of our time reconnecting after finally seeing each other in person again. Throwing on my coat, I walk outside into the crisp morning air, where Demon waits in his car."Goodmorning," I say to him with a bright smile. He simply lifts his chin at me. He doesn't seem to be a man of many words."So," I say after getting into the car, deciding to talk to him anyway. "What's your real name? Calling you Demon doesn't feel right to me.""No one calls me by my real name.""That's fine. I'll just give you a nickname. How about D-bug? It suits you. Bugs can be scary but they're pretty cool once you know more about them," Demon sends a look that way and I know he's annoyed."So, D-bug, what have you been up to.""My names Dominic," He begrudgingly gives in.The rest of the ride I try to make talk with him but his answers are rarely more than three words. After a while, I give up on making conversation and soon after that we arrive at Leah's bookshop. It's technically just called The Bookshop, but Leah's so well known around every refers to it with her name. As soon as I open the door, Chris and Leah are hounding me."Are you okay! Do you need more time off! I didn't get to thank you for the Christmas tree," Leah takes me into her arms and squeezes the life out of me and I wheeze as all the air in my lungs rushes out. Like always, her blond pixie cut is disheveled."I'm fine. It was just a break-in," I say when she releases me. Silas said that I can't tell anyone what's going on but I feel bad lying to them."Who's this," Chris says, eyeing Demon in a not-so-friendly manner. This confuses me because he almost looks jealous. He's shown no sign of liking and he's had girlfriends in and out of his life since I've known him. Still, I can't help but feel flattered. I quickly scold myself for thinking that, there is no way Chris wants anything to do with a girl like me."This is Dominic. He's a friend of mine and he's going to be accompanying me to work until this whole thing blows over," I tell him, not wanting to give to much away. He still eyes him untrustingly and Dominic returns the look."Thank you for looking out for our girl! I'll get you a cupcake on the house. You look like a red velvet type of guy," She says, leaving before he can protest. One of the main appeals of Leah's Bookshop was that she brought in baked goods every week. Leah's wife, Kristy, baked them every night. Last week it was cinnamon rolls. Leah brings Dominic his cupcake and we open up the shop. The customers start to pick up later in the day. Word got out that it's cupcake week and it seems like the whole town is here. Chris is on cupcake duty so I help people find and buy books. Dominic sits at the little coffee nook, looking bored out of his mind. I'm sure spending his day in baked goods/bookshop was never something he saw himself doing. Chris keeps close by me the whole shift and puts his hand on my lower back whenever we pass each other. It's almost possessive the way he hovers over me. I even catch him sending a glare towards Dominic a couple of times. When my lunch break comes I decide to keep Dominic company while Chris takes over the shop."I know you're bored to death. As payment, everything's on the house for you," I say, sitting in front of him, vanilla raspberry cupcake in hand. "Sorry about Chris this morning. I have no idea what his deal was.""He likes you," Dominic says simply."You think so? There's no way. I've known him for years and he's shown no signs of liking me," I try not to give away my crush on him by blushing."He feels threatened by me. He's probably been comfortable knowing he'll always have you as an option when he decides to give you the time of day. Now he thinks I've ruined that for him."I'm pretty sure my eyebrows are touching my hairline. Firstly, this is the first time I've heard Dominic say more than one sentence. Secondly, I'm surprised he really believes that Chris likes me. Anyone with eyes can see the difference between us. Chris looks like he could be in a Calvin Klien ad. Meanwhile, I'm just chubby and average looking."You can't be serious. Chris could have any girl in the world if he wants to. Why would he get jealous over me?""Don't talk about yourself like that," He says it almost like an order and his jaw gets hard."You don't have to flatter me, Dominic. I have eyes.""Well, they must not be working right. Since I've been here I've seen about ten guys flirt with you and I stopped counting after a while," I'm pretty sure my cheeks are on fire. I think back to all my interactions with male customers and none of them seem any more than friendly."We'll have to agree to disagree," Dominic looks like he wants to say more but he doesn't press the issue. By the time my break is over, I've finished my cupcake. The rest of the day flies by and soon Chris, Leah, and I close shop. Like always, Leah let's each of us take home the leftover goods. When I leave the shop, Dominic is already waiting by his car for me.On the way home, I turn on the radio to fill the silence in the car. I know Dominic doesn't like the girly pop song station I put on, but he'll just have to deal. Dominic looks relieved when we reach the house. I wave at him from the front porch when he drives off but I do think he sees it."You brought snacks," Mia says excitedly as soon as she spots the pink box in my hand."Cupcakes. Leah always lets us take home the leftovers.""Everyday? I can't deal with that kind of temptation! It would go straight to my ass," Mia pouts. Mia's slender frame isn't an accident, she goes to the gym most mornings. I wonder how she does it, mornings already kinda suck and adding exercise seems like a form of torture to me."Well, you need it. Your back is looking a little long," I joke. Mia sends a glare my way but she knows I'm kidding.Like always, we spend the afternoon watching sitcoms on the couch. Mia gives in and has a coconut cupcake. Silas comes home later that evening and they both go in their room, to do god knows what.That night I dream about red velvet cupcakes and Dominic's forest green eyes.

FIve Chapters posted! Yippee!

Turn that little star orange for some good luck!

Chapter Six

Sephie's POV"Are you even listening, Mia?" I ask, annoyed. Her eyes are fixated on the computer screen, browsing facebook."I was!" She says, quickly closing the laptop. I roll my eyes and continue."You promised you would go to the movies with me! It's starting in an hour and we need to get ready," I pout at her. We've been planning to see the newest romantic comedy together for days but it's just like Mia to completely forget. I'm surprised she even remembers her own name at this point."I'm sorry, Sephie. Silas is taking me out tonight. He's been working a lot lately and we haven't been out in a while," Mia says, looking genuinely apologetic. I'm still annoyed and if I'm honest, jealous. All she talks about is Silas and now she's ditching me for him. I miss the good old days when I could have a conversation with my own sister without her mentioning some stupid boy."Fine! If you wanna ditch me, I'll just go by myself," I grit out."You know you can't be out alone. I'll text Demon.""I'm not a baby! I can go by myself," I say, wanting to stomp my foot. Every time I want to go anywhere, Dominic has to be there. "Not happening," She goes back to scrolling through Facebook.I storm off to my room, feeling like a petulant child. I set aside a cute outfit for our outing but now it feels stupid since it's just going to be me and Dominic. Not to be mean, but the guy's a drag. Since that day at the bookshop, I haven't been able to get more than a sentence at a time out of him. I decide that I'm going to get him out of shell today.When I leave the house, I send a glare at Mia just so she knows I'm still angry. Dominic is already outside, leaning against the car. He must live nearby because it never takes him less than ten minutes to get here whenever I need an escort. He opens the door for me like always and get's in after me."I hope you know I'm in disagreement with this. I am an adult and I should be able to leave the house by myself," I tell him, still feeling pouty."You have an Mc on your ass over fifty thousand dollars," I pout again because I know he's right. I can't stay mad long because as we approach the theater I get excited. I stare in excitement at all the movie posters lining the theater walls."That's the one!" I point out the movie poster to Dominic, though I'm sure he couldn't care less. The leading actress and her love interest are in a loving embrace in the middle of a busy city street. I stare at it with hearts in my eyes. I'm a romance fanatic, whether it be in film or in romance books. Ever since I was a little girl I loved watching two people fall in love. It gave me hope that I'll have my own love story one day.I rush out of the car, not waiting for him to come around and open my door, which he's insisted on doing. When I open the doors the smell of fresh popcorn makes my mouth water. Dominic catches up to me and grabs my arm."Don't run ahead of me like that. You could've gotten hurt," He apprehends grumpily. I roll my eyes at him and slide my hand into his and drag him along. His hand is warm and big against mine and makes slightly flustered and I let go of it as soon as we get to the snack line."Can I get a large popcorn, an orange soda, and a bag of gummy worms," I ask the lady at the concession stand. When it's time to pay, Dominic reaches for his wallet."You don't have to," I tell him. He gives me a look that shuts me up and I let him pay.I almost skip to our section of the theaters. The theater doesn't have many people and I choose the seats in the very back. Dominic sits next to me and I wait for the commercials to end so we can watch the movie.The movie starts and I watch in wide-eyed excitement as the opening credits roll. Soon I'm captured by the characters budding romance.Dominic's POVSephie sits next to me, eyes fixated on the screen as she shovels popcorn into her mouth. I'm a little annoyed at being dragged to some chick flick, but my mood can't help but be lightened by Sephies brightness. When she slid her hand in mine earlier I felt a strong surge of protectiveness over her. Her hand felt so soft and fragile.I can't deny that I'm attracted to Sephie. I catch my eyes lingering on her soft curves and gentle smiles all the time. The other day at the bookshop I watched her happily interact with all the customers, oblivious on the effect she had on every man around her. Bitter jealousy filled me when I noticed the way she blushed around her coworker, Chris. When she made those horrible comments about herself I wanted to stomp right over to him in the middle of that bookshop and kick his ass. Anyone lucky enough to have the attention of Sephie should be forever thankful. That's why I've been trying to distance myself from her. I know I can never have a girl like her, my darkness will end up corrupting her. My attraction to her goes beyond physical and I want to make her mine so bad it hurts.When the movie ends Sephie gushes like a teenage girl all the way to the car. Even though I don't act like it, I hang to her every word. Chick flicks are not my thing but if she likes them I'll sit through one hundred just to be close to her."Wasn't that so romantic. He was so head over heels for her. I wish someone will love me like that one day," Her voice is wistful and eyes dreamy. Her words make me angry. She's so oblivious to how she attracts everyone around like a moth to a flame. If I could have her I would treasure her for every second of my life. At that moment, I know I have to make her mine or at least try. Maybe It's selfish but I have to be the one to have her. There's no way I can leave after she's safe again, knowing she'll probably end up with someone like Chris. I know she can't handle my darkness but I can hide it from her.When we arrive at Silas's house, I know he's not there because his car is gone. Sephie has fallen asleep next to me, head leaning against the window. I walk around to her side of the car and pick her up. Her head leans against my shoulder and I feel intense protectiveness over her. I carry her inside and into her room and lay her down in bed. Putting the covers over her I stare at her sleeping features, transfixed. Her long eyelashes cast a shadow over her cheeks from the moonlight coming through the window. I brush her curly hair back before leaving.As I leave I decide that tomorrow will be the day that I make sure everyone knows she's mine, including her.

That star looks a little lonely down there...maybe if you gave it a little tap you can brighten its day.

Chapter Seven

Sephie's POV

I wake in the middle of the night from the intense urge to pee. Maybe guzzling all that orange soda wasn't the best idea. I don't remember arriving home so Dominic must have carried me in. I grab my phone to see the time it's about two in the morning so I must have been asleep for two hours.Getting up, I do my business in the bathroom and go to the kitchen to get a glass of water. I glance out the window and sure enough, Silas and Mia are still gone. I don't even want to think about what they're doing out at 2 a.m. As I'm grabbing a cup from the cabinet I hear something fall and break in the living room."Dominic," I call out, confused. When I get no answer I get scared. I put the glass down and look for a weapon, grabbing a fork from the utensil drawer. It's not much but I can poke somebody's eye out with this. I slowly walk from the kitchen into the living room and scan the area. I see no one, but a vase that was on the coffee table is knocked over and the window is open. Terrified, I run back into the kitchen and pull out my phone and speed dial Dominic. "Sephie? Are you okay?" He answers groggily on the third ring."I think someone's here. The window is open and a vase is knocked over," I say in a shaking voice."Fuck! Is Silas there?" He asks, sounding wide awake now."No, he's still out with Mia. I'm so scared," I say, almost in tears. I remember what that man said he wanted to do to me and I'm terrified that he might follow through. He probably wants to kill me for hitting him with that vase."I'll be there in five minutes, Sephie. Stay on the phone with me. Do you have a weapon?" He asks. I tell him about the fork I'm awkwardly holding in my hand."I'm coming down your street right now."I wait for Dominic to come, terrified that someone is in the house right now, waiting for the perfect moment to murder me. When I see headlights in the driveway, I run out the front door, desperate to be safe in Dominic's presence. He's out of the car as soon as it's at a stop and I throw myself into his arms, sobbing into his chest."I was s-so scared!""It's okay now, Sephie. No one's going to hurt you," His words wash away all my fear and we stay like that until I stop crying. I follow Dominic into the house and he surveys the scene, checking every room to make sure nobody is here."Somebody definitely came in through the window, the screen has been cut through. They must have left when they heard you call me," He says, examining the window. He calls Silas and gives him a run of the situation. About fifteen minutes later, Silas and Mia arrive, looking worried."I'm so glad you're okay," Mia says, pulling me into her arms."I'm taking Sephie home with me," Dominic says. All of our attention is on Dominic, surprised."Silas, you're too busy with Mia and running your business to protect Sephie. She needs to stay with someone who can give their full focus to protecting her," My jaw falls open in shock. Why would Dominic care enough to have me stay with his? Most of the time he seems annoyed with me."You don't need to do that, Dominic," I tell him, not wanting to burden him."He's right, Sephie," Silas speaks up. "You'll be safer staying with Dominic. You could have been seriously hurt today.""I agree," Mia says. I'm still uncertain. Dominic has already gone out of his way to be my personal bodyguard. At the same time, I know that I'll feel safer with him. His presence always makes me feel protected. Also, I don't think I can sleep here knowing someone broke in."I'll go," I concede. Silas and Dominic discuss things while Mia helps me pack. I don't have much so it all fits into the duffle bag she let me borrow. When it's time for me to leave, Mia pulls me into a tight hug."I shouldn't have left you," She says, sounding guilty. I don't think she's just talking about today. I know she feels like it's her fault all this is happening because she left me with mom."None of this is your fault. I couldn't have asked for a better sister," I squeeze her one more time and Silas sends a nod in my direction before I go. I put my duffle bag in the backseat of Dominic's car and get in.It's after 3 a.m and the slow rumble of the engine lulls me to sleep. Before I know it, I'm taken out of my slumber by Dominic lifting me out of the car and into his arms. Being in Dominic's arms makes me feel safe and content. He lays me in a bed and I snuggle into the soft sheets. I'm asleep almost immediately.***The sun shines in my eyes, waking me up. I'm confused for a second by the strange room but I remember what happened last night. I'm staying with Dominic now. The room looks masculine and neat, a bed and a dresser with mahogany floors and grey walls. The wall by the bed has a large window and the sun brightens the room. There is a bathroom connected to the room, complete with a modern-looking shower and sink. I stay in the shower for nearly thirty minutes, soaking under the warm spray from the showerhead. When I get out, I notice my duffle bag on the floor beside the dresser. I unpack and take out a pair of leggings and a hoodie. I put my damp curls in a messy bun, and leave the room.The rest of the house is the same, masculine, sleek, and modern. I would have expected Dominic to be messy since he was a boy, but the house is spotless to the point that you wouldn't think anyone lived there. The kitchen looks expensive, sleek steel appliances and black marble. I make my way back to the livingroom but jump when I feel a furry head brush against my leg.It's the cutest little kitten I've ever seen, with grey and white stripes and big greyish blue eyes. He purs again, staring up at me with wide eyes. I'm a sucker for kitties, I've always wanted one but my mom was allergic. I kneel down and rub his soft fur, cooing at him."What's your name, little fella?" I ask him. He purrs again as I scratch behind his ear. "That's Rocky. I found him in my backyard and decided to take him in," I jump at Dominic's voice and my mouth goes dry at his appearance. His dark hair is wet and hanging around his face and beads of moisture stick to his torso. He's in a pair of sweats and his muscles are clearly on display.

My eyes follow one of the beads of moisture and I feel the intense urge to taste them."Oh," Is all I can respond with, my brain mush. I can't imagine Dominic saving a little kitten and naming it Rocky. Maybe I misjudged him because of his badass reputation. The more I get to know him I'm starting to see a softer side to him.I watch awkwardly as Dominic opens a can of cat food and puts it in Rocky's bowl. He scratches him behind the ear a couple of times and Rocky leans into his touch."What do you want to eat?" He asks, looking through the refrigerator."You don't have to cook," I say. I'm surprised he even offered, most guys I know can't even bowl water."Do you want to cook?""Now that you mention it, It's best if you do the cooking around here," I say. Anytime I've ever tried to cook anything it's ended in disaster. I have a short attention span so I burn everything. I even burnt soup once, leaving it on the stove and forgetting about it after getting engrossed in a T.V show.I'm surprised at how much of a good cook he is when he slides the steaming plate in front of me. It's an omelet with mushroom, onion, and spinach. The flavors are perfect and my eyes nearly roll to the back of my head in pleasure."This is good! Where did you learn to cook like this?""I had to cook for me and my little sister when I was younger," He answers. I had no idea he had a sister. In fact, I don't know much about him at all. I want to ask more but then I remember something."I'm supposed to be at the bookshop today!" I exclaim. In the stress of yesterday, I forgot all about my job. Leah and Chris probably think I'm dead right now."You need to stay here until all this blows over.""You can't be serious?! I love working at the bookshop," I pout."Whoever broke into the house knew you were there. They might be following you," My face pales at his words. They might have already seen me at the bookshop then. The last thing I want is to put anyone else in danger."We need to tell Chris and Leah. It's only fair they know, now that this affects them too," Dominic's jaw gets hard at the mention of Chris's name."You can fill them in over the phone," He agrees.After washing our plates, I call Leah and fill them in on everything that's been happening. Of course, they both freak out and I'm pretty sure Chris has a seizure. I'm relieved when the call is over. Although they're a little betrayed that I hid this from them, It feels good to finally be able to tell them the truth.

Turn that little star orange for some good luck!

Chapter Eight

Sephie's POVI stare out the window at the outside scenery. The sun is just starting to set and all shades of pink, orange, and red paint the sky. Dominic and I are leaving from Mia and Silas's house after having lunch there. The whole time Mia gave suggestive looks towards me and Dominic. Even though it was annoying, I couldn't help but be flattered that she thought I was the kind of girl that Dominic would go for. Dominic's probably into long-legged modelesque girls who could pull off the whole seductive look. Not too old to be old virgins who've never even been kissed before.As we leave their neighborhood I spot the top of a Ferris wheel peeking out from the tops of buildings. I immediately perk up, remembering that this is the time of year when our city sets up the fair."Dominic, look! There's a Ferris wheel!" I screech. Dominic nearly swerves the car at my sudden outburst. "You have to take me! Pretty please? With a cherry on top?" He looks annoyed but gives in, making a u-turn. I bounce up and down in my seat, feeling like a kid on Christmas morning."I'm gonna text Chris and see if he wants to meet us there," Dominic looks even more annoyed as I pull out my phone. Chris responds fairly quickly and says he'll meet us by the front gate in twenty minutes.When we approach the fair I want to dance around in excitement. I wait for Dominic to open the door for me even though I'm nearly bursting with excitement. The smell of delicious food and sounds of chatter and music fills the air. Dominic insists on buying my ticket and we wait out front for Chris to arrive. As soon as I see his lean blond figure I jump up and down, waving at him excitedly.Chris's jaw clenches when he spots Dominic. If looks could kill, Dominic would be six feet under and so would Chris because he's returning the look. When Chris is close enough, he pulls me up into a tight hug and spins me around."It's good to see you, Sephie," When he finally puts me down he places a kiss on the top of my head. I'm pretty sure my cheeks are actually on fire. Although Chris and I have been friends for years, he's never shown this type of affection towards me. Dominic grabs me around the waist, almost possessively and shoots Chris a look that could make a grown man shake with fear. Though I really doubt either of them has a crush on me, I'm sure they must really hate each other.Even though both of them are acting like jerks, I still manage to have a good time. I'm terrible at all the games but Dominic and Chris give me everything they win. I end giving a lot of it away because I have so much stuff that I can't carry it all. Whenever I want to buy a snack or something, Chris and Dominic nearly fight each other to pay the bill. I think their rivalry must be some alpha male thing.It's time to get on my favorite attraction of the fair, the Ferris wheel. I excitedly run towards the entrance to the ride and the line is very short, only about four people. When we get there I notice that each carriage only seats two people. This get's my spirit down a little bit, I was really looking forward to riding it with both of them."Only two of us can get on," I pout."I'll get on with you," Chris volunteers before Dominic can even get a word out. Dominic's jaw tightens, but Chris is already grabbing my arm and dragging me to the empty carriage. I feel bad leaving Dominic there but the excitement of the ride gets me giddy again.The ride starts and soon we're overlooking the whole city. I've never been afraid of heights, It's always given me a rush to be so close to the sky and far from the ground. By now the sun has set and the fluorescent lights of the fair makes everything look so magical."That Dominic guy is starting to show up everywhere you are. Are you guys seeing each other?" Chris asks. I'm confused, he's never shown any care for my love life."No, he's just making sure I'm safe until this whole thing blows over.""I could do that. You don't even know that guy," Chris says, lips tight."This has all just been so sudden. I have a bunch of bad guys after me, I've been moved from my mom's house to Mia's, then to Dominics. I just-""You're living with that guy!" Chris exclaims, cutting me off."I told you about the break-in, Chris. I couldn't stay there," I'm confused about why Chris is acting this way all of sudden."You could have stayed with me! I looked this guy up and he's bad news. His street name is Demon and he's a damn underground fighter!""What's your problem, Chris? You've been being a jerk a lot lately," I say, starting to get angry. I just wanted to enjoy a day at the fair with my friends and he decided to start a fight."My problem is you, Sephie! I like you and I know you like me, too. I didn't want to tell you at first but then all this shit happened and now you're seeing this Dominic guy. I just- fuck," Before I can think, Chris crashes his lips against mine. I'm in complete shock as his lips move roughly against mine, nearly bruising them. Then I'm angry. I pull away roughly and my hand sharply connects with his cheek."Dominic was right. You've been stringing me around this whole time," I'm so angry and hurt that tears gather in my eyes. He's been flaunting all his girlfriends around me all the while he knew how I felt about him. I'm also embarrassed. Of course he knew, everyone knew. I acted like a complete mess whenever I was around him, stumbling over my words and getting flustered."Sephie, I'm sorry," Chris says, sounding genuinely apologetic. I don't care about his apology though. I just want to go home.As soon as the ride ends, I'm out, nearly sprinting away. Dominic grabs my arm before I can make my escape."What's wrong? Did that asshole hurt you?" Chris asks, looking so murderous even people passing by look scared."You were right about him," I say simply, tears falling down my cheeks. Chris finally catches up with me but before he can plead for my forgiveness again, Dominic has him by the collar of his shirt."I would kick your ass right now but you're lucky it would scare Sephie. If I see you anywhere near her again you won't be so lucky," With that, Dominic lets him go and Chris stumbles back. Dominic grabs my hand and leads me away from the staring onlookers and into the parking lot where he helps me into the car. By this time I'm full-on crying. My friendship with Chris is probably ruined and I'm humiliated that he knew I had a crippling crush on him this whole time. "He doesn't deserve your tears. You're too good for him," Dominic finally speaks up when we arrive at his house."Everyone knew how I felt about him. I feel so pathetic, having a crush on a guy so far out of my league.""You have no idea, do you," Dominic says."About what?" I ask in confusion."The effect you have on everyone around you. You're oblivious to it.""You don't have to flatter me, Dominic," I say, not believing a word of it. I still can't believe that Chris liked me. He must have felt sorry for me."You're so wrong about yourself, Sephie, and I'm going to make you see that," Before I can even process what he said, he gets out of the car, leaving me dumbfounded.

As always, give that star a little tap!

Chapter Nine

D ominic's POV

I knock on Sephie's door only to hear her muffled dismissal. She's been locked in her room since the situation with Chris happened last night. My jaw tightens when I think about how much he hurt her. When I found out that he tried to kiss her I wanted to hunt him down for causing Sephoe pain. Also, I have to admit, the thought of someone other than me kissing her grates my nerves. Sephie's too good for him and it hurts to know that she can't see that about herself. She deserves someone to treasure her and put her above everything else and I'm going to be that guy.

I hear my phone ringing in the other room and pick it up off of the living room table. The caller ID says Silas, so I know it's important.

"What's up?" I answer.

"Mia and Sephie's mom just tried to contact Mia. She says she needs her help and wants to meet up," I tense up in anger. Her mom is definitely up to no good, no mother who would put her daughter in this much danger has an ounce of good in them.

"She probably knows she's in trouble now. Have Jackson find where the message is coming from. Once we get the 50k from her the MC won't be trying to hunt Sephie down."

I'm familiar with the club that Sephie's mom stole from, in fact, they wanted me to work with them at one point. My refusal angered them and the fact that I'm now protecting the girl they want to hunt down doesn't help.

"People are talking and apparently if you don't give Sephie over they're gonna start problems."

"If they want to get Sephie they're gonna have to get through me," I say, meaning every word. Even though I haven't known her for long, I've never felt the way I feel for her about anything.

"She's yours?" Ace asks.

"Yeah, she's mine."

"Then they'll have to get through me too."

After our phone call, I go back up to Sephie's room and open the door. I know she's still hurt by what happened yesterday but she needs to talk to someone about it. She's laying in bed, facing the opposite direction of me, curls all over the place and in a pair of sweats and a sweater. I sit next to her on the bed next to her and she turns to face me.

"What do you want," She grumbles. Her eyes are rimmed red from crying.

"You've got to get out of here. You haven't eaten all day," I tell her.

"I'm fine. We both know I don't need it," My jaw clenches. I hate it when she talks down on herself, especially over that boy.

"Don't talk about yourself like that. You need to take care of yourself and eat something."

"Why do you even care," She says angrily. "You just feel sorry for me just like everyone else. You don't even like me."

"That's not true. I care because I see how beautiful and wonderful you are and I hate it when you talk down on yourself."

"What do you mean," She asks, brow furrowing.

"I want to make you see yourself the way I see you. I want to be the one who makes you feel beautiful and I want to do it every single day."

"I-I don't know what to say," She stutters out, eyes wide.

"You don't have to say anything right now. Let's just get some food in you," I say getting up and reaching my hand out to Sephie. She takes it and I lead her into the kitchen.

***

Sephie's POV

I'm in utter shock as I follow Dominic into the kitchen, my small hand cradled in his large one. How could Dominic like me? He's all tall and handsome and I'm short and chubby. He can get any girl he wants so why does he feel this way about me? I come to the conclusion that he and Chris feel sorry for me. There is no other explanation.

Dominic sits me down at the counter and pulls out a bunch of ingredients, seemingly for a soup. I can't help but watch him as he makes it, mesmerized. He's gorgeous, green eyes contrasting so beautifully to his black hair, focused on the task at hand. He's so tall and muscular that even I feel small compared to him even though I'm far from it. I can't deny the way I feel around him like I could before he said all those things to me.

Dominic sets the steaming bowl of soup in front of me, along with a tall glass of water. I dig in, and as soon as the flavor hits my tongue I realize how hungry I am. Before I know it the bowl is empty. I blush at the fact that I just pigged out in front of Dominic.

"Drink some more water," He urges. He fills my bowl again and I dig in again, being more mindful to not look greedy. When I'm done he puts everything in the sink.

"Would you like to watch a movie?" Dominic asks.

"What?" I'm surprised that Dominic wants to watch a movie with me, just a while ago he seemed annoyed by my presence.

"You said romance movies always made you feel better."

"Oh-uh okay," I say, shocked that he'd want to sit through a cheesy romance with me.

Dominic and I sit on the couch and he opens Netflix. Rocky jumps up onto the couch next to us, kneading the cushion with his little paws before curling up in a tiny ball of cuteness.

Dominic lets me pick and I choose one of my favorite romance movies. It's dark when it starts and I'm a little nervous, sitting so close to him. I can smell his cologne and his arm is pressed up against mine. I start to loosen up when I get engrossed in the movie.

As the movie goes on I find myself naturally leaning against Dominic and soon enough his arm is around my side as I lean my head against his should, legs folded under me on the couch. I don't even remember how we got like this and I don't want to think about what it means but it feels so good. His body is hard against my softness and I find myself sinking into him. His hand comes and stroke hair and my eyes close in pleasure. I feel all fuzzy inside being like this with Dominic and it scares me to no end.

I wake up with Dominic's hand around my waist. We are both laying on the couch, on our sides, my back to his front. There's a warm blanket over us and the movie has long ago turned off. Rocky lies at the end of the couch by our feet, fast asleep. I must have fallen asleep like I usually do during movies. I know I should wake Dominic up so we can both go to our own rooms but I just can't bring myself to do it. It feels so good to cuddle up next to him and I never want to leave. I snuggle deeper into his arms and drift back off to sleep, feeling safe and protected in his arms.

I hope you guys liked this chapter!

Chapter Ten

"Holy shit! Who is this, Dominic?" I'm awake immediately, torso off the couch, along with Dominic. Our sudden movements scare Rocky and he jumps off of the couch. There's a girl in the house, standing at the end of the couch. She's short, even shorter than me and my 5'2 is already considered below the average height. Her inky black hair is long, falling in messy waves down her back and her eyes are almost like Dominic's, except slightly more jade than forest green."Shit, Dee, you can't just barge in here like that!" Dominic bites out. She looks totally unfazed by his anger, which is impressive because Dominic is can be intimidating."You shouldn't have given me the key, then. Now, who's the girl?" She askes, giving a pointed look in my direction."I'm Sephie. It's nice to meet you," I speak up. She's obviously related to Dominic, she looks like the female version of him and I'm positive Dominic wouldn't be taking so kindly to a stranger barging into his house."What a beautiful name," She says with a bright smile. "I'm Delilah, but you can call me Dee. So, how long have you and my brother been seeing each other?"My cheeks heat up as I realize how bad this looks. Dominic and I were just sleeping together on the couch, his arm wrapped around my waist. Of course, she thinks I'm his girlfrie nd."Jesus, Dee, you just met the girl. Give her a break," I'm surprised he didn't outright deny that he was dating someone like me."Well, I'm going to need an explanation. You've never even bothered to bring a girl home and all of a sudden your cuddling on the couch with someone."Dominic's never brought a girl home? He must be the hit it and quit it type of guy because I'm sure he doesn't lack female attention."Look, why don't we talk about it over breakfast? Sephie and I should go get dressed," Dominic says, ending the conversation. Dee reluctantly agrees to pause her interrogation and we both go to our rooms to get dressed. As soon as my bedroom door closes behind me I'm in freak out out mode. I just met Dominic's freaking sister! And it happened in the worst possible way ever! I decide I have to make a good impression from now on. I want to look good, but also casual, so I put on a sued brown skirt and cream sweater. I top it off with some booties and let my curls frame my face. They're a mess, so I have to fluff them out a few times before it looks right. I leave the room, hoping I didn't take too long. I can smell bacon frying and hear it sizzling in the pan. Dominic is cooking and Dee is sitting at the counter. She waves me over and I sit next to her."Dominic filled me in on your situation, and boy do you have bad luck," She tells me."You're telling me," I joke."I don't buy the whole 'moving you in for your protection' thing. I know my brother and he wouldn't do that if he wasn't head over heels,""Dee!" Dominic scolds, giving her a pointed look. Dee drops the issue but looks like she wants to say more. I want to tell her nothing is going on between Dominic and me but she seems so excited that her brother is 'head over heels'. I'll just let Dominic break it to her.Over breakfast, I learn that Dee is the polar opposite of her brother, which, no offense to him, is a little refreshing. She's outgoing and goofy compared to Dominic's intense seriousness and several times I found myself almost spewing orange juice out my nose at her humor. I even caught Dominic chuckling a few times."You banned her from her job! She has nothing to do, Dominic. Lord knows being stuck in a house with you all day isn't the most exciting thing in the world," Dee exclaims. I was telling her about Leah's bookshop and the fact came up that I'm not supposed to go there."It isn't safe," Dominic says, looking like there's no way he's budging on the subject."Why don't you go with her like you did before?""No. End of conversation," Dominic says sternly."Oh, that's bull. You just want to keep her all to yourself, don't you? That's so unfair!" Dee exclaims. Dominic ignores her and I sit there awkwardly, both Dee and Dominic look hard set in their stances and I don't really feel like I have a say."Since you don't want to let Sephie out, I'll just bring the outside world in. Sephie, give me your phone," I have no idea what she has up her sleeve, but she looks no-nonsense so I quickly comply. She types stuff for a few seconds before handing it back to me."There. Now I have all of Sephie's friends numbers. If you don't let Sephie go to the bookshop, I'll have no choice but to invite all of them over every day in protest to annoy the heck out of you," Dee says with a smirk. Dominics composure cracks and he looks a little horrified at not only having to deal with Dee but all my friends every day."Dee, you're overstepping boundaries," Dominic tells her."And you aren't? Did you even think about how Sephie feels about all of this," Dominic looks a bit guilty at that."Fine. Three days a week though, that's all," Dominic gives in. Dee gives a big holler of happiness and I feel a bit better that I can go to the bookshop now. To be honest, I'm really starting to miss that place."See, Sephie? You can't just let this big grouch run all over you," Dee says, nudging me under the table. Later on, I wave at Dee from the driveway as she drives off in her miniature red sports car. Even though we didn't meet in the most tasteful way and she is a little crazy, I did enjoy her company."Remind me to change the damn locks," Dominic mutters grumpily when we come back inside."I think your sister is really cool," I tell him truthfully."Just wait until you have to deal with that, every day, for years on end," Dominic says, still looking grumpy.The rest of the day I spend with Dominic and I start to warm up to him a bit more. I get a little flustered still, at the way he's been acting around me lately. When he walks past me now he naturally puts his hand on my lower back or shoulder, which always sends shivers down my spine. When sitting on the couch with me, he puts his arm around my shoulders and even tucks me into his side sometimes. I try to rationalize all this in my head. Friends cuddle sometimes, right?At the end of the day, once again I find myself being carried to the bedroom, having fallen asleep on the couch during a movie. I feel him brush some loose curls from my forehead before leaving me in my room. I kind of miss falling asleep cuddled into his chest, but I ignore the feeling.When I fall asleep again, I dream about Dominic and how his lips would feel against mine.

Ten chapters uploaded!

As always, Turn that little star orange if you liked this chapter!

Chapter Eleven

I help Leah give out the free cookies, which has drawn a large crowd in the bakery. They're shaped like little snowmen, which I think is adorable. There's only a little time left until Christmas and Leah wanted to give our customers a little treat. When people saw the free cookie sign they almost broke down the doors at opening time. Leah's wife, Kristy, is helping out today since the crowd is so big. Chris has been giving me space, but he does send sad looks at me every so often. I ignore them, still angry about what happened at the Fair.Dee decided to stop by and so did Mia, so they ended up hitting it off immediately. This scares me, being that they are almost exactly alike and I've already dealt with Mia my whole life, I can't handle two of her. I can swear Dominic looks smug at the fact that I'm probably going to be stuck with Dee now, too.When It's finally time for my lunch break I take a seat next to Dominic in the coffee nook."Our sisters are teaming up against us," I tell him, sending a pointed look towards them chatting on the other side of the room, clutching their sides with laughter."I can see. If this gets any worse we'll have to move across the country.""Are you gonna eat that," I say, pointing at the cookie across from him. He slides it my way and I devour it in less than half a second. I would be embarrassed but Dominic doesn't seem to mind me pigging out."I can't believe you aren't eating these. I should have Leah send me the recipe.""From what your sister's told me, I don't want you anywhere near my kitchen," Dominic says."What did she tell you! I only ever set something on fire once, and wasn't even my fault," I say, defensive. Ever since I accidentally started a grease fire, Mia swears I shouldn't be within two feet of a flame. Dominic ignores me, clearly not believing a word."I should make some tonight, just to prove you wrong.""I won't be there tonight," Dominic responds. I'm a little disappointed, used to spending my days watching romance movies on the couch with Rocky and Dominic. "Why," I pout."I have a fight tonight," My heart drops in my chest a little. I've been so busy living in la-la land with Dominic that I've forgotten that he has a whole life of his own. A criminal one at that."Can I go?" I ask with pleading eyes. I don't know the ins and outs of underground boxing but one thing I do know is that it's dangerous. I couldn't sleep tonight knowing that Dominic might be getting hurt."Absolutely not," Dominic says, jaw tightening. I remember Dee telling me to stand my ground to get my way with Dominic but I want to try another approach. I try to pull off the best puppy dog look I can, eyes wide and pouting lips. Dominic shifts a little in his seat but doesn't give in."Please?" I pout. Dominic runs a frustrated hand through his hair."Fine! But you don't leave my side or do anything I don't tell you to do," Dominic gives in. I squeal like a girl and clap my hands together, earning some strange stares from customers. I guess Dee was wrong about how to get my way with Dominic.Dominic drives me home from the Bookshop, and I'm excited the whole way home. I really want to see this side of Dominic life. Even though his fight is later tonight I start getting ready as soon as we get home. I don't want to dress up too much, it's an underground fighting ring and I doubt many people will be dressed to the nines. I decide on a pair of dark wash jeans and an old band tee, putting my hair in a messy bun on my head. Dominic rolls his eyes when he sees me."We're not leaving until hours from now," He tells me. I plop down on the couch beside him."I just want to be prepared," I say. He mutters something along the lines of 'I should've never agreed to this' and goes back to watching his sports. That's one thing about Dominic,

Although he lets me watch whatever cheesy stuff I want on most days, he won't change the channel for anything when a game is on. I guess he deserves it, sitting through all my girly romance movies. The rest of the day, I sit tucked into Dominic's side, while he focuses intently on the game. Even though It's pretty boring and I have absolutely no idea what anyone is saying, It's nice to just be near Dominic. I know these feelings are wrong. They'll only get me hurt and I shouldn't indulge in them but I just can't help it, I've never been attracted to anyone the way I am to Dominic. Chris never even gave me these feelings.When it's finally time to leave, I follow Dominic outside to the car, Nervousness kicking in. I'm silent the whole ride, imagining what seeing Dominic fight will be like. I don't want to see him get hurt and I have never been a fan of violence.Dominic and I arrive at what looks to be an abandoned warehouse. Dominic comes around to open my door and I nervously follow him to the building. As soon as he knocks, A huge bald man opens the door, He gives Dominic a nod and we walk in. I hear the muffled sounds of a huge crowd as he leads me down a dark hallway. When he opens the double doors, the sound is amplified by a thousand. I've always been nervous and claustrophobic in large crowds. A group of men, one of them I recognize to be Ace, meet us there and lead us through the crazy crowd. I rub my sweaty palms against my shirt, ignoring all the eyes on us. Dominic said there would be a lot of people but I didn't know it would be to this magnitude. There are hundreds of people and you can't even get anywhere without bumping into a body."Dominic! I fucking love you!" I hear someone scream. I look up in surprise only to meet eyes with a gorgeous girl with silky black hair. She sneers at me, the clear question of what I'm doing with Dominic on her face. In fact, many people look at me that way and I know I look like a sour thumb, the short chubby girl in a room full of people who could be models. I wish I listened to Dominic and stayed home. I don't belong here and I don't belong in his world.They lead us to a part of the room sectioned out from the crowd, where only a few people stand. As we break through the crowd I notice that in the middle there are two men already fighting. I'm amazed at the sight, they throw punches like they want to kill one another."Oh my god," I gasp when one of them throws a sickening punch, some of the other guy's teeth clattering to the concrete floor."It looks bad but most of these guys are used to it," Dominic comforts me."What if that happens to you?" I ask, worried. Seeing Dominic get hurt would kill me."I won't let it. I promise," He tells me. "I have to go get warmed up. There's going to be three more matches before I come out. Stay right here. If you need anything, call Ace."Before I can wish him luck, Dominic leaves, going around the crowd and out through a door which is blocked off from the crowd."Is that your man?" A voice asks from behind me. She has long dyed red hair that is in two french braids, and pale skin covered in tattoos. She too is in the sectioned off area and I assume she knows one of the fighters."Oh no! We're just uh..." I trail off, not really knowing what we are. "The 'no labels' type, huh," She says, giving me a knowing look. "I've dealt with one of those before. That's my man over there, in the black shorts." She points him out and he's the one who knocked the guy's teeth out."Do you come here a lot?" I ask."Yeah. You have to get used to all the groupies. Not a lot of girls can handle being with a man who gets all that attention," My heart drops the harsh reality. Every girl in here would probably kill to spend one night in Dominic's bed. I can't compete with that."I'm Terry, by the way,""I'm Sephie," I tell her. After a while, I get used to the fighting happening before me. I'm no longer scared but fascinated by the technique and how focused the fighters are on defeating each other. I'm not prepared, though, when Dominic comes out. His dark hair is put back in a ponytail and he's in dark blue boxing shorts. Everyone screams his name, even louder than when the other fighters were making an appearance. His opponent is shorter than him, but buffer, with thick muscles and veiny arms and his hair is in a buzzcut. His eyes are intent on Dominic, sharp and intense."Ladies and gentlemen, the undefeated Demon!" The announcer yells to the crowd. They go crazy, there screams so loud it's deafening.My heart pounds fearfully in my chest as I watch Dominic make his way to his opponent.

Chapter Twelve

I completely understand why people call him Demon now. Dominic pounds on his opponent, with absolutely no mercy. The other guy is strong but Dominic is strong and fast, hitting him with a series of punches before he can even get one hit in. I thought I would be terrified, seeing Dominic in such a dangerous situation, but I'm turned on by this and I feel a little sick admitting it to myself. I've always cringed at violence but seeing Dominic so unhinged, almost primal, is the most erotic thing I've ever experienced. Sweat beads on his chest as he lays punch after punch. The fact that I'm getting any pleasure out of this level of violence is shocking and I wonder if all this is even real but the dampness between my legs leaves no doubt this is reality. The crowd begins to cheer Dominic's name as the end of the match comes near. His opponent is getting weaker, punches coming in slower. For a split second, he leaves his face vulnerable and Dominic takes his opportunity to land a sickening uppercut. My jaw drops as his opponent's feet lift off the floor at the power behind the punch. He's out cold and for a second I wonder if he's seriously injured. Dominic kneels down and puts his hand to his face. I'm confused but then I realize he's making sure the guy is still breathing. "Damn. That's one man you got there," Terry says next to me, looking on in amazement. I don't respond, too shocked at the scene in front of me. I feel a strange sense of pride at

Dominic's win, amazed at how skilled he is in his field.Dominic makes a beeline towards me as the crowd cheers his name. He's even more attractive up close, his chest shining with sweat and hair clinging to his face."You look like you just saw a ghost," He bends down to whisper this in my ear. I can feel the heat radiating off of him and his warm breath tickles my ear."I-uh..." I trail off, brain a pile of mush."You'll get used to it. I think I like having you in the crowd. It makes me want to impress you.""Yo u...want to impress me?" I ask, utter confusion marking my features."Of course. Maybe then you'll let me have you," My jaw hits the concrete floor. My brain refuses to process what he just said, deciding instead to completely shut down. Dominic chuckles."Let's go home. We're skipping the after-party," Dominic says. He wraps his arm around my waist, hand resting on the curve of my hip, and leads us away. His boys come too, protecting us from the crowd. They can't protect us from the obscenities they shout, though, and I hear every single word."Demon, I want to have your babies!""I'll suck your dick, Demon!""Why are you with that fat bitch?!"I cringe at the derogatory terms they throw my way. The fact that the girls shouting them look like models doesn't help. They look like the type of girls that belong on Dominic's arm, beautiful and seductive all at the same time. I look up at Dominic's face and he seems totally unaffected by their words.When the door closes behind us I sigh in relief. Although it's much better here, their screams are only muffled from outside the building. We're in a locker room and several fighters are there in various states of undress. My whole face warms up and I try to avert my eyes. I sit on the bench as Dominic goes through his locker, taking out several items of clothes along with a towel."I'm going to take a quick shower. If someone messes with you, tell them you're with Demon," Demon leaves to the stalls, which is on the other side of the locker room. I've never felt so awkward in my life, stuck in the middle of a men's locker room. I stare at my fingernails, not wanting to look up and acknowledge all the stares I'm probably getting."What're you doing here, sugar," A man asks, smirking down at me. He has on basketball shorts and a t-shirt, tattoos covering one arm, and his dirty blonde hair is shaved in the back but long in the front, hanging over his forehead."I'm uh- with Dominic," I say, remembering his words."Oh, you're one of his girls, huh? Seems like he's going through one every week," He says. My heart sinks in my chest. Dominic really has a new girl every week. Since the day of the fair, I may have deluded myself into thinking there was some small, microscopic chance that Dominic liked me. His words confirmed my fears, I was just a pathetic ugly girl who fell for someone way out of her league. "I'm not like that," I bite out. I want to run out of here but I have nowhere to go."There's no need to lie about it. How about you show me what's got Demon going crazy over a girl? He doesn't let anyone call him by his real name so your pussy must be made of gold," My cheeks burn at his suggestive words. Just as I'm about to book it out of here, not caring that I have nowhere to go, Demon has him pinned against the lockers."What the fuck did you just say to her," Demon growls."Hey, chill man. I was just talking to her. It's not like she's your girl or anything," He says it jokingly but his voice trembles."She's fucking mine! If you ever even look at her again I'll make you wish you never met me," Dominic's anger sends chills down my spine. Why did he say I was his? He must be doing it just to make a point to this guy. I shouldn't get my hopes up, I'll only get hurt in the end."Alright, it's all good man," He says, fear now clearly in his voice."Fucking apologize," Dominic forces him to face me."I'm sorry! Just let me go!" Dominic lets his collar go and the man stumbles."Get the fuck out of here," Dominic snarls. He grabs his stuff off one of the benches and high tails it out of the locker room. We've gained the attention of pretty much everyone in the room and I just want to go home and forget this ever happened."That goes for all of you. Sephie's mine and if you disrespect her, you disrespect me," Everyone in the locker room gives Dominic a nod of respect. He leads me out the back door of the locker room to avoid the crowd and I'm in complete shock and confusion. Everything that comes out of Dominic's mouth seems to contradict how he feels about me. He obviously doesn't like me, he's way out of my league, but he acts like he wants to be with me I'm starting to get frustrated. It seems like he's purposely leading me on. He knows what happened with Chis, so why would he manipulate my feelings like that."What was that about?" I question him after we both get in the car."No one messes with what's mine," He tells me and I lose it. "What's yours?!" I quote him, yelling. "Why are you doing this? Stop leading me on. We both know you don't like me. Everyone knows! You heard what they said in there, you're way out of my league, so please stop pretending that you want to be with me."Before I can even think, Dominic grabs my shoulder and pulls me toward him, his lips crashing against mine. Naturally, I put my hand on his shoulder as his lips move roughly against mine. I can't think about anything, except how good his lips feel, rough yet gentle, taking yet giving. Before I can think logically, my hands are threading through his long hair and my lips reciprocate his actions. I moan as our lips dance together, heat gathering in my core. Dominic roughly pulls away, and I'm left there gasping, heated and confused."Now do you believe me? I fucking need you, Sephie, in my bed and by my side."

They finally had their first kiss!!! If you liked this chapter, please leave a vote or comment.

Chapter Thirteen

I'm still in shock when we arrive at the house. My lips are swollen from our kiss and I have no idea what to think about any of this. There is no way I can rationalize this in my head. The only thing I can come up with is that Dominic is a psychopath womanizer who takes pleasure in making elaborate schemes to win the hearts of insecure mediocre women, only to break them when he gets bored. This is obviously far fetched but it's slightly more believable than him wanting to be with me.

Dominic comes around to open my door and leads me into the house, hand on the small of my back. When we get in front of the door to my room he leans down and places his soft lips to my forehead.

"I know this is a lot for you so we'll talk in the morning."

With that, he leaves into his own room and I stand there in shock for a second. My mind is blank as I take off my clothes and get in the shower. My thoughts start racing when I lay in bed. I can't sleep, running over the events of today, trying to find a way to rationalize them. The worst part is the little glimmer of hope blooming in my chest. I don't find sleep until the sun is just starting to rise outside my window.

***

I wake up in the early afternoon, still feeling exhausted. I haven't slept in this late since highschool. Throwing on some clothes and putting my curls in a bun, I make my way into the living room, expecting Dominic to be there. To my surprise, he's nowhere to be seen. On the counter, there is a note and I pick it up and read it.

Went to the gym, will be back at 3 pm. We'll talk then.-Dominic

I'm relieved that the talk he said we will have is postponed. I go about my day for a while, having a bowl of cereal and responding to texts. Then I get restless. Without Dominic here there is nothing to do. I decide to call Mia and see if she can come over.

"Hey, Sis," Mia answers.

"Are you busy today? Dominic left and I'm bored."

"Not at all, Silas is working today. I'll call Dee and we'll come over for a girls day!" Mia says excitedly. I roll my eyes, Dee and Mia are already partners in crime. We hang up and I wait for them to come over, bored out of my mind. When I see their car pull up in the driveway I excitedly open the door before they even get to it.

"Okay, spill the tea," Dee says as soon as she crosses the threshold of the door, immediately going to the fridge.

"About what?" I ask, confused. I'm not usually up to date on gossip.

"What's happening between you and my brother. There has to be something, he doesn't just let anyone call him by his real name. Other than you, my mom and I are the ones allowed to call him Dominic," Dee and Mia plop down on the couch, several snacks in hand.

"There's nothing. Dominic and I are just friends, that's all," I state, face heating up as I sit down next to them. I just wanted them to keep me company but it backfired and now I'm being interrogated.

"Bull. I've known you my whole life and you don't even light up around me the way you do around him," Mia tells me. "Now let me and aunt Dee in on the tea. We won't tell a soul."

I'm hesitant at first but I really do need some advice about this whole thing. I know Dee is Dominic's sister but Mia wouldn't bring her here if she thought she would say a word of any of this to Dominic. So I sit there on the couch and tell them everything, from what happened at the fair to yesterday and all my doubts. They both listen intently, not interrupting. When I'm done there is a short moment of silence.

"Sephie, are freaking crazy?!" Mia exclaims.

"What?! No," I say, offended.

"Dominic literally spelled it out for you and you still can't see. No man goes this much out of his way for a girl he thinks of as a friend. He freaking kissed you! You have to be out of your mind if you interpret that any other way."

"Maybe he just feels sorry for me. When he met me I was all banged up. He probably feels some obligation towards me. I know you guys don't want to hurt my feelings, but I am obviously not the type of girl Dominic would go for," There's another moment of Silence and both Dee and Mia are looking at me like I've just sprouted another head.

"So, you're blind and crazy. Great," Dee mutters.

"Sephie, do you really think that about yourself," Mia says, sounding disappointed.

"I know you're my sister so you'll always see me as beautiful, but there's obviously a difference between me and you. You've always gotten all the attention and I'm just seen as your fat sister," I tell her. I feel a little relieved when I get it out. I feel like this has always gotten between us a bit. I love Mia, but I can't help but feel inadequate around her. If I'm telling the truth, that's why I avoided coming to see her all this time. I feel bad just thinking it, it's not her fault that I'm jealous of her.

"You're beautiful, Sephie! And you get attention too, you're just too insecure to notice it."

"Dominic would be lucky to have you and I know this because I'm his sister," Dee tells me.

"You need to let your walls down and let Dominic in. You'll never be happy if you're always running from everyone because you think you're not good enough. Believe me, I know. I wouldn't let Silas in because it was hard for me to trust him but now that I did, I've never been happier," Mia says.

It's hard to admit it, but maybe they are right. I've always been so insecure about myself all my life and it's hard to see myself any other way and even harder for me to believe that anyone else does. Maybe Dominic does want to be with me. Right now I may not see why but Mia is right, I don't want to sabotage every chance of being happy because I can't see through my own insecurities.

"You guys are right," I tell them.

"Trust me, we know," Dee says, with a smile.

"Now, give Dominic a chance. Even if it doesn't work out, you need to be more comfortable with getting yourself out there," Mia says.

Dee and Mia leave before Dominic gets home, knowing about the talk we're supposed to have. I stand on the porch and watch as their car drives away. When it's out of sight, I come back into the house, letting out a sigh. Even though their pep talk made me feel better about talking to Dominic, I'm still terribly nervous. Will Dominic want to be with me? Even though the thought is unbelievable, it still sends a thrill of delight through me.

When Dominic's pulls in the driveway, I nervously jump up, instinctively going towards the door to open it. I stop myself, not wanting to look like I was waiting for him. I play it cool, turning the T.V on and sitting on the couch. When he comes in I act natural, like I haven't been pacing back and for for the last hour. Dominic is in a pair of grey sweats and a teeshirt. He looks freshly showered and when he sits next to me I get a whiff of his body wash and it makes my stomach flutter.

"How was the gym?" I ask awkwardly. Less than twelve hours ago we were making in the driveway and now he's sitting right next to me.

"It was fine. I have to train more, I have another fight coming up."

"Really? Tell me about it," I ask. I'm stalling a bit but I'm also interested in what he's talking about.

"I'll tell you about it later. Right now we need to talk," He says and a rush of nervousness goes through me.

"I know you've probably already made something up in your head about what happened last night which is why we should've had this talk this morning. I meant every single word of what I said. I've never felt for anybody what I feel for you. Every time I'm in the same room as you it takes all my self-control not to take you then and there. I want to protect you, even from yourself and all the terrible things you think about yourself. You may not know it yet but you're already mine, you've been mine since I first saw you."

Dominic's intense eyes are in me the entire time he talks and I feel like I'm going to melt under the heat of them. His words confirm what Mia and Dee said earlier. He really feels this way about me.

"Why me? You could have any girl you want, so why do you want me?" I ask.

"Maybe I can have any girl I want but none of them are you. You're the only one who can make me feel the way I do, no one else has ever made me feel this way. Sometimes I think I'm losing my sanity when I'm around you. Only you have ever made me lose this much of a grip on myself and it drives me fucking insane that you can't see it," Dominic growls the last part, hands running through his hair in frustration.

"I feel the same way about you. I've never felt this way about anyone, either. I still don't see what you see in me but I know that I want to be with you," It's all out there now. I avoid Dominic's eyes, feeling vulnerable. I've never been this open with anyone about my feeling, let alone a man. My cheeks are on fire and I feel the terrible fear of rejection. What if he likes me but doesn't want commitment?

"Look at me," Dominic orders. I bring my eyes to his and I'm sure he sees the fear swimming in them.

"Fuck," He mutters. His lips crash against mine and this kiss is more heated than last, both of us desperately moving our lips together. My fingers thread through his hair as his lips roughly take mine. He bites my lower lip and his tongue runs across it, sending a shiver of pleasure down my spine. I open my mouth and his tongue snakes in, thrusting against mine. I moan, following his motions with mine. His groan sends a thrill through me, the fact that I'm having the same effect on him as he has on me makes me feel like the luckiest woman alive. My hands trail down to his shoulder, feeling the bulging muscles there, as our tongues move together.

When we pull apart both of us are breathing hard. I'm pretty sure my panties are soaked. I have never felt that level of desire before. At that moment while we were kissing, I wanted him to take me there on the couch. I still do but I know that I'm not ready for that yet.

"Fuck, Sephie. It's taking everything in me not to take you here and now."

'Do it' I say to him in my head. Of course, I don't have the balls to really say it. Although hormones are clouding my head right now, I still have a small bit of sanity left.

"Does this mean..." I trail off.

"You're mine, Sephie, and I'm going to let the whole world know."

Looking into his eyes, I know a whole new world has begun for me.

Chapter Fourteen

I sit next to Dominic in the bookshop's coffee nook. His arm is wrapped around my side and I'm completely pressed up against him. At first, I was nervous at the public display of affection. We got a bunch of stares from all the customers, wondering what the chubby girl who gave them book recommendations was doing on the arm of a man who could be a male model. Leah looked like she could just burst with happiness when we walked in together, hand in hand. Chris, on the other hand, looked at me in betrayal and hurt. I almost feel guilty, but he did this to himself. When he gets his head out of his butt and apologizes, maybe we can think about repairing our fractured friendship.

"Can I get you another cake pop?" The new server asks. Since I've been gone a lot since the break-in and business is picking up for the holiday season, Leah's hired a new girl to pick up the slack. She was one of the people looking at Dominic and me in confusion when we came in together. She's tall and slender, with long blonde locks and freckles spattering her nose and cheeks.

"We're fine, but I'll take some coffee," Dominic tells her. Her cheeks get red at his attention and I can't help the jealousy bubbling in me. If Dominic has girls like this blushing over him, how can I compete? She fills his cup with black coffee, cheeks still cherry red.

"I'm Caroline, by the way. I just started today," She says nervously, attention on Dominic, completely ignoring me. Jealousy rears its ugly head and I feel anger bubbling in my gut. Doesn't she see him with me? Get a freaking clue.

"Thank you, Caroline," Dominic says in an obviously dismissive way. I want to laugh in her face, but I know it's wrong to feel that way. Jealousy is such an ugly emotion and I'm usually not like this.

"Is this your sister?" She asks, giving a quick hopefull glance my way. My cheeks burn, in anger and humiliation. Is this how everyone will always see me and Dominic? We look nothing alike, I'm black and Dominic is white. Also, I don't know any brothers who hold their sisters like this.

"She's my girlfriend, obviously. You're only one day into your job and you're already being rude to customers. I'm sure Leah wouldn't be too happy to hear that, seeing as Sephie is her favorite employee," Dominic tells her coldly.

"I am so sorry. I-I'll go. Please enjoy your coffee," She stutters out, then scuffles away. I'm happy that Dominic told her off but I still feel shitty that this even happened at all.

"I know what your thinking, Sephie, and you're wrong," Dominic tells me, noticing the look on my face.

"I can't help it. This is all so new to me and it's going to take some getting used to," I tell him softly and his eyes get gentle.

"I know and I'm going to be there every step of the way."

I wave to Leah as Dominic walks me out the door. I huddle into my sweater as Dominic opens the car door for me and I wait for him to get in. The car ride isn't silent, we talk about everything from our taste in music and our favorite books. The more I get to know Dominic and his personality the more I like him. It scares me to no end, being so open with someone.

When we arrive at Dominic's house I notice a minivan in the driveway. Mia and Dee don't drive it and I'm sure that's not the type of car Dominic's friends would drive.

"Fuckin' hell," Dominic mutters under his breath.

"Who is that?" I ask curiously.

"That's my mom's car. She always comes around for Christmas. I'm sorry, Sephie, I forgot," Dominic explains.

"Oh my god! Your mom is here?!" I exclaim, starting to freak out. The woman who gave birth to Dominic is here! I pull out the passenger window, making sure my curls aren't to wild.

"You look fine, Sephie. Mom's going to love you. She's been on my back about settling down, so don't be surprised if she asks you about her future grandkids," Dominic tells me, getting out of the car and coming around to open my door. My hands are sweating as we make our way up the driveway and I wipe them against my jeans. This all so sudden, me and Dominic just began our relationship and I'm already meeting his mom.

"Dominic, dear! Is that you?" I hear her call from the kitchen. The smell of cinnamon and vanilla permeate the room and I know she's baking something delicious.

"Oh my! Who is this young lady?" She says when she comes from the kitchen. Her raven hair is cut in a bob and her eyes are a deep-sea blue. She slightly pudgy and she's wearing denim jeans and a blue blouse to match her eyes. The laugh lines around her mouth make her seem friendly, and you can tell she laughs a lot just by looking at her. I wonder how Dominic ever became so rough growing up with this woman.

"Mom, this is my girlfriend, Sephie," Dominic introduces her. He might as well have told her he just won the lotto, the way her eyes light up.

"I never thought I'd see the day! She's just beautiful, perfect for you," She says, coming over and pulling me into her arms. I'm extremely flattered that Dominic's mom thinks I'm perfect for him.

"It's so nice to meet you, Ms. Hayes," I tell her.

"You don't have to be so formal, call me Judy," She says, letting me go and smiling up at me. She's just as short as Dee.

"You should have called, mom," Dominic chides.

"You know I come here every Christmas. My flight back home isn't until the night after Christmas," She says.

"Sephie will put her things in my room. You can take the guest room," Dominic tells her. A little thrill goes through me at the thought of sleeping in the same bed as Dominic. This is happening so fast and I don't know if I can help it.

While Dominic's mom takes whatever she's baking out of the oven, I transfer my clothes from the guest room to some of the empty drawers in Dominic's dresser. I can't help but admire his room, having never been in here. The walls are grey and the floors monogamy, matching the theme of the rest of the house. All of his clothes are folded neatly, each drawer holding specific items. It still surprises me how neat and organized Dominic is. When my eyes travel to the bed a blush covers my cheeks. Tonight, I'm going to be sleeping in there with Dominic. The thought sends a shiver down my spine and I quickly leave and go back in the kitchen.

"The cookies are cooling. Why don't you help me get dinner started, Sephie?" Judy asks.

"Sure, but I have to warn you, I'm not the greatest when It comes to cooking," I warn her.

"I'll teach you! Come, we're making lasagna," Judy says, motioning to the ingredients scattered across the counter.

I actually learn a lot, cooking with Judy. She chats away and I'm relieved I don't have to do much work to carry the conversation. When we pull the pan out of the oven, I'm proud of our work. It smells delicious and the melted cheese makes my mouth water. Dominic helps us set the table and put food on the plates. My stomach is loudly grumbling by the time we all sit down in front of our meal.

"This is delicious, Judy," I say in surprise after I try the delicious cheesy goodness.

"Well, you helped make it, dear. You have to have some cooking skills if you want to feed my future grandbabies," My cheeks warm up at her remarks about grandchildren.

"Mom!" Dominic chastises.

"Just putting it out there. I'm only getting older and I want some grandchildren before I'm too old to play with them," She says.

Judy doesn't make any more comments about grandchildren for the rest of the dinner. She and Dominic catch up and I learn that they don't have much family other than themselves. I know Dominic's dad isn't around and I have a feeling that's a sensitive issue with them. I help Judy clean the kitchen when we're through and afterwords she retreats to the guest room, saying she's tired from the jetlag.

I'm nervous as I make my way to Dominic's room. I have zero experience with the opposite sex so sleeping in the same bed with Dominic seems out of this world. I remember the few times we fell asleep together on the couch watching movies but that was different. This seems so much more personal. It feels like Dominic and I are moving way too fast and we're in so deep even though this is only the beginning. For a second I want to cop out and tell Dominic I'm spending the night on the couch, but I brave it out and approach the door.

I take a breath before opening the bedroom door, trying to calm my racing heart and soothe my nerves. I know Dominic is in there, waiting for me and that just gives me even more anxiety. I've never been in any situation like this and I don't know what to do with myself. I give a quick prayer before turning the cold metal door nob with my sweaty hands.

Chapter Fifteen

A/N: Some NSFW things happen in this chapter . If that makes you uncomfortable, please skip ahead.

I don't actually see Dominic when I get inside the room but I can hear the shower running in his bathroom. I awkwardly wait on the bed, nervously playing with my fingers. I hear the water stop and moments later Dominic emerges, a towel wrapped around his waist and water beaded on his broad chest. I blush, I'll get used to seeing Dominic this way. I quickly grab my clothes and go into the bathroom to give him privacy.

The bathroom is still steamy and the smell of his body wash fills the room, making my mouth water. His shower is even better than the one in the guest room, the water seems to jet from every direction. The only soap in here is his masculine body wash and the smell of it is so him, oaky with a tang of spice.

I step out of the shower and dry up, putting on the shorts and tee-shirt I picked out. I put my hair in a pineapple on the top of my head and leave the restroom. Dominic is already in the bed and I slide in next to him, feeling so nervous at being so close to him, in bed and under the covers. Before I can even get a grasp on myself, his arm wraps around my waist, pulling me towards him.

"Fuck, you smell like me," He mutters, face buried in the crook of my neck. My cheeks are fifty shade of red, and I let out a gasp as his lips lightly brush over my neck. A shiver runs down my spine.

"Dominic," I whisper huskily at him.

"I fucking need your mouth right now but I don't know if I can stop once I have it," He tells me. I don't what comes over me, maybe a momentary loss of sanity, but without thinking I pull his face to mine and press my lips against his. There's nothing stopping us, we're in his bed, alone, and his mom may be in the other room but the walls are thick, she won't be able to hear a thing. I want Dominic in every way and I know we just got into this but I trust him with every part of my body.

Dominic rolls on top of me as his lips take mine his hips positioning themselves between my legs. My core clenches at the hard bulge pressed against me, right there, exactly where I need it to be. Lust takes over and I push up against him and groan at the sharp pleasure that shoots through me.

"I need to stop," Dominic says once he pulls his lips away from mine, both of our breath coming out in gasps.

"Honey, that's the exact opposite of what I need you to do right now," I tell him. I push my hips against him again, the pleasure even sharper this time.

"Fuck, you're going to fucking kill me, Sephie," Dominic's groans, voice sounding almost pained. I continue to push my hips up against his, all thought process out the door. My mind is completely tuned into that place between my legs and every time I move against that bulge pleasure shorts through me. My cheeks are flushed and my nipples are hard, my whole body aches with desire. In the back of my mind, I'm embarrassed at how I'm acting. Dominic probably thinks I'm a sex freak now.

"Sephie," He groans my name and for the first time, he pushes back against me. My back arches and unbelievable pleasure shoots through me. His lips trail against my neck, kissing and sucking, leaving hot trails of pleasure where ever they go. I'm totally at the will of the thrusts of Dominic's hips. That bulge feels harder and more strained than it was before and every thrust takes me higher and higher.

"Dominic!" I call out as I reach the very precipice of pleasure. I shake as I fall, pleasure shooting through me. My fingernails scratch at Dominic back through his shirt. I have never felt this level of pleasure before, and if Dominic can bring this out of me just by grinding against me, fully clothed, I wonder what other pleasures he can bring me. My moans die down as the pleasure subside and I feel like I've just run a 5k.

"Oh god," I moan out in embarrassment when the reality of what just happened hits me. I just attacked Dominic like a madwoman while his mom is in the other room.

"Fuck, Sephie. I have never seen anything so hot in life," Dominic tells me, face buried in the crook of my neck. I notice that he's still rock hard against me.

"Dominic, you didn't..." I trail off, too embarrassed to say it.

"I'll be fine," He says, rolling off me.

"That looks pretty painful," I say, motioning towards the bulge that can be seen even over the covers. "Let me take care of you. You did the same for me, It's only for."

"I don't think you're not ready for that this early in the relationship. I'm happy with just giving you pleasure. In fact, what just happened was the best experience of my life." He tells me. He pulls me against him but our hips our separated so I won't be pressed against his bulge. My head rests on his chest, his arms around my back.

"But Dominic-"

"I'll be fine. Now, go to sleep," He orders, softly. I'm tired from what just happened and I find myself blinking as my lids start to feel heavy. I feel warm and snuggly against Dominic's chest and the sound of his breathing lulls me to sleep.

***

Dominic's POV

I sigh in relief when Sephie falls asleep against me. The bulge in my pants aches in unbelievable ways and if I don't take care of it now I'm not liable for what I might do. I thought I had died and gone to heaven when Sephie thrust her hips against mine. It was a task not to cum in my pants like a little boy as I ground into Sephies softness. When she came, shaking against me, It took every ounce of self-control I had not to take her then and there. I know she would have let me, the little vixen. My kitty showed me how she purs today and I'll never forget it.

I carefully leave the bed, mindful not to wake her up, and go into the bathroom, closing the door behind me. As soon as I have privacy, I pull my out my aching member, desperately needing relief. As I stroke myself, I think of Sephie. Her soft curves, wide hips, the curve of her belly, her smile, her chiming laughter, her moans. Every single thing about her that's so damn perfect to me. Just thought of her sets me off and I explode, groaning in pleasure. Afterward, return to our room and slide back into bed. Before

I can go to sleep, my phone rings and I reluctantly pick it up from the nightstand. I groan when I see Austin's name on the screen.

"What is it," I bite out. It's late and he knows better than to call me at this time.

"Dane dropped out of the fight," He answers and I curse. Sephie sturs so I quiet down.

"I have been fightin' for you for years. I can't get a fuckin' break every now and again?" I curse.

"We don't have anyone else willing to go up against Devil. This is our New Year's fight, you'll make big money, so much that you can retire if you win," He tells me. He has my interest then. Devil, just like me, is undefeated. People will spend anything on a fight this big. And I like the idea of retiring, this whole underground fighting world is getting old. Now that I have Sephie in my life (and I don't plan on that ever changing) I know she won't be pleased with me having to train all the time.

"I'll do it. I'll fly over there after Christmas," I tell him.

"You need more time to train, Demon. This is going to be the biggest fight of your career."

"I'll train here in the meantime," I tell him. He reluctantly agrees. He's the best trainer there is and I'm going to need all the prep I can get.

After putting the phone down, I slide back into bed with Sephie and pull into my arms, her head resting against my chest, my arm around her back. She unconsciously snuggles into me, burying her face in my chest. I can't help but admire how beautiful she is, those curls, her cute little pert nose, and plump lips. I thank the heavens that I was lucky enough to get an angel like her. What a bastard like me did to deserve it, I'll never know, but I won't question it. I drift off to sleep while gently stoking Sephie's back.

Sephie bout to get that D. I'm so proud of her

Turn that little star down there orange if you liked this chapter

Chapter Sixteen

I wake up early, just before the sun is rising. I'm surprised that Dominic's side of the bed is empty and I hear the shower running in the bathroom. I sleepily sit up in the bed, pulling the covers around me. My eyes go to the slightly ajar bathroom door and my stomach clenches. It's open just enough that I can see the mirror above the sink and reflected in it is Dominic, eyes closed, head tilted back as the spray of water rinses the foamy soap off of him. The glass shower walls are fogged up with steam, but I can see his broad muscled chest clearly and just barely, the v-line above his pelvis.I avert my eyes, feeling like a creep. The water stops and moments later Demon emerges with a towel wrapping around his waist."Goodmorning, beautiful," He says, placing a kiss on the top of my head. My cheeks warm, not used to this type of affection. It's still hard to believe that we're together, as a couple."Goodmorning," I tell him. He walks over to his dresser and I avert my eyes before he drops his towel. Embarrassed, I head into the bathroom, making sure to close the door behind me all the way. I brush my teeth then I quickly strip and get in the shower, again using Dominic's body wash. When I get out I notice that I forgot to bring a change of clothes in. This means I'm going to have to go in there only wearing a towel. I've never been that bare in front of someone, especially Dominic. My body isn't like the ones Dominic is probably used to seeing, I don't have a thigh gap and my stomach isn't flat. My thighs and butt are chunky and I have cellulite and stretch marks. The towel doesn't hide any of this and I'm afraid that if Dominic sees it, he will reconsider wanting to be with me. I make sure to avoid meeting Dominic's eyes when I go into the room, hoping he doesn't notice me, but his sharp intake of breath assures me he does. The dresser is right in front of where he's sitting on the bed, now fully clothed. I try to ignore him as I go through the dresser, knowing there is probably a look of disgust on his face. I surprised when his large hands grip my hips, pulling me toward him and sliding up to my stomach. "Are you purposely tempting me?" He purrs in my ear. My breathing comes out shakily, feeling naked with his hand on my belly. I feel his hardness pressed against my backside and I gasp. I can't help but feel flattered that he still desires me, even after seeing me in this state of undress. "N-No," I sputter out, taken by surprise. I feel the same heat I felt yesterday building in me. "Hmm... It seems like it. You're lucky I have a place to be, beautiful, because if not I would have to teach a lesson about teasing me," With that he lets me go, leaving me extremely turned on and dazed. I quickly grab an outfit and rush into the bathroom, wondering what Dominic's idea of teaching me a lesson is. I get dressed in a flash, putting my hair in the usual messy bun because I'm too lazy to do anything with it. When I emerge from the bathroom Dominic is on the phone. I catch the end of the conversation before he hangs up. I heard enough to catch that he plans on leaving after Christmas. "Where are you going?" I ask him, sitting down beside him on the bed. "I have a fight on New Years'. It's in another state and my trainer is down there," He tells me. "Can I go?" I pout at him. I haven't been separated from him since the break-in incident and the thought of being away from him is almost painful. "No. My concentration has to be completely on training, this is a big fight for me. If you haven't noticed, you're kind of a distraction to me," I pout again at the part about being a distraction but he stops me before I can say anything."A good distraction," He assures me. "I'm not leaving until after Christmas. I'll call you every day and you can stay at your sister's house until I come back.""Okay," I give in reluctantly. To my surprise and delight, he pulls my chin up to him and softly rubs his lips against mine, the faintest hint of a kiss."I have to go to the gym," He tells me, sounding reluctant to leave."Am I banned from tagging along there too?" I ask and he chuckles."No, you can come if you like. There's not much to do there though," He warns, amused."Watching you get all hot and sweaty? That sounds like something to do to me," I blush as soon as the words leave my mouth but Dominic throws his head back and laughs."My little kitty's a feisty one," He purrs. "We better leave now because if we stay in this bed any longer I might never let you leave."Even though I like the sound of that, I allow him to lead me out of the room and we drive to his gym.***I watch as Dominic throws punches at the heavy bag, eyes intent on it as if it were his prey. He's just in a pair of basketball shorts, his muscles gleaming with sweat. My mouth waters at the view and I shift in my seat. I can't believe I get to call that hunk of sexiness mine.When we arrived, I was surprised that Dominic's gym was the same place he had the fight. Now that it wasn't packed to the brim with people, I could appreciate the facility. You'd expect a place like that holds underground boxing matches to be dirty and moldy, but it was well kept and clean. In the gym area, there were other fighters training, some sparring with each other, but I noticed that Dominic kept to himself. There were a couple of other ladies there, who I assume were there for their boyfriends. I noticed Terry's bright red hair right away and sat next to her. There's not much conversation between us as we both intently watch are men train."All this sexiness is making me light-headed. I'm going out for a cig," Terry tells me after a while. I give her a slight smile as she gets up and then my eyes are back to Dominic and I'm drooling againBy the time Dominic finishes training, It's almost early afternoon. He approaches me, wiping his sweat with a white towel. "Did you enjoy the view?" He asks with a devilish smirk."It was okay," I say, pretending to sound unimpressed. I can't control myself at his boyish look of disappointing and I burst out in laughter."What did I tell you about the teasing," He says and his heated look shuts me up. Then he's the one laughing and I'm still flustered."I'm gonna go take a shower and change in the locker. I'll be right back," He says, placing a kiss on my forehead. I watch him disappear out of the door. There's a little flutter going on in my stomach at his public display of affection. Dominic keeps proving me wrong every day. Not only does he like me but he seems to like showing me off and he wasn't put off by my body this morning. This all seems unreal, like the romance stories I read and watch in movies. I can't help but feel like this is too good to be true and I'm in for a rude awakening.Dominic emerges from the locker room and we walk out of the gym hand in hand. He opens the door for me, as always, and we drive back to his house in comfortable silence. When we walk in I can smell something cooking and Dee is here, chatting in the kitchen with her mom."You lovebirds left early. Sephie, why don't you help us with lunch?" Judy asks, eyeing Dominic possessive hand on the small of my back with pure joy.Cooking with Dee and Judy is fun and I can see where Dee gets her sense of humor from. Under Judy's guide, I'm starting to get better at cooking and when we all sit down to eat, I feel a little pride well up in my chest at Dominic's enjoyment at the food I helped cook. ***It's late in the evening and all of us are sitting on the couch, watching a cheesy Christmas movie. I feel bad for Dominic, not only does he have to live in a house full of girls but he's forced to watch our girly shows. He does look slightly annoyed, but also a little bemused whenever we get emotional during the sad scenes. I'm sitting with my head leaning against Dominic's shoulder, petting Rocky who is curled up in Dominic's lap when my phone interrupts the movie."I'll go take this," I say getting up, not wanting to distract them during the movie. Closing the door behind me in Dominic's room, I answer the phone."Hello," I say. There is a long period of silence and I say it again. When there is no answer I hang up, creeped out. I'm about to go back into the living room when the same number calls again."Who is it," I answer again, slightly annoyed now."Sephie..." My mother's voice, raspy from years of smoking, finally says and I nearly drop the phone in shock.

Chapter Seventeen

A /N: This chapter contains mature sexual content, read at your own discretion.

"Mom..." I whisper, completely taken by surprise."You ungrateful child! After all the things I've done for you, you haven't even tried to help me!" She nearly yells in my ear. My teeth clench at her audacity to be angry at me."After all you've done for me?! You could have gotten me killed!" I angrily hiss at her. She's already put me in danger and If they find out she's communicating with me they're going to think I know where she is."Do you know what I've been through? You're living it up with your little boyfriend while I have a motorcycle club after me," I stand in stunned silence for a while. "How do you know who I've been staying with? And I have to stay with him because your little friend broke into the house!""This isn't about that, Sephie. I need your help," She says, ignoring my questio n."You've gotten me in enough trouble," I tell her."Sephie, all the money is gone. If I don't pay them, they'll kill me.""You gambled it all away already?!" I ask, stunned that she could blow through all that money so quickly. Her silence answers my question. "I don't have fifty grand lying around to give you. You dug this hole for yourself, Mom.""What kind of daughter are you? They'll kill me if I don't get them the money. You're just going to leave me to die?" I feel a twinge of guilt at her words."Your boyfriend is a big-time underground fighter. He has a big fight coming up, he'll probably make a ton of money. He trusts you, you can get the money from him and he won't even know you did it.""You can't be serious..." I whisper. She's actually suggesting I steal from Dominic. The thought makes me sick to my stomach."If you don't they're going to kill me and it's going to be your fault."I jump at the door opening behind. Dominic is standing there, a look of worry on his face."Is everything okay? You've been in here for a while," He says."Think about what I said, Sephie. I'll talk to you later," She says in my ear before hanging up."I-I was just talking to Mia," I say, putting my phone back in my pocket. I feel bad for lying but I don't want him to be worried. He looks a little skeptical, but he doesn't press the issue and we both go back into the living room to finish the movie.I'm nervous the whole time, shifting in my seat. Dominic can tell something is off about me, shooting me a couple questioning looks that I pretend to ignore. After the movie ends Dee, Judy and I start dinner. The whole time I can't concentrate, and when we sit down to eat I don't even taste the food. Eventually, Dee goes home and Judy retreats into the guest room. By the time I get into Dominic's room, he's already showered. I quickly get in the shower to avoid Dominic and I purposely take a long time, soaking under the warm spray of water until my fingers are pruned. I change into some sweats and a t-shirt and join Dominic in bed. I lay on my side, facing away from him, hoping he won't ask any questions."What's going on with you, Sephie?" Dominic asks, seeing through my facade."What do you mean?" I ask, trying my best to sound innocent."Don't lie to me, Sephie. I can something is wrong with you," He grabs me by the arm and forcing me to face him."It's just..." The heated look on his face makes it impossible for me to lie to him. "My mom called.""Jesus, Sephie," He growls, sitting up in the bed. "Why didn't you tell me?""I just...I didn't want to worry you.""What did she say to you," He asks."She gambled all the money away and now she can't pay them back. She knows that I'm staying with you right now and she wanted me to..." I pause, scared of what Dominic will think."What did she want you to do," Dominic says, face darkening. I gulp before continuing."She wanted me to take money from you so that she could pay back her debt," I say, nervously waiting for his reaction."Sephie," He sighs. "You should have just told me.""I know," I admit, feeling guilty."I'll try to find out where she called from. Next time something like this happens, tell me," He says sternly."I'm sorry. I just don't want you to be burdened with all my problems." I say, looking away. Dominic grabs my jaw and pulls my eyes back up to him."I'm not burdened with your problems. I care about you and I want to protect you," He tells me, looking intently into my eyes. His green eyes are heated and full of so much emotion that l feel like he's looking into my soul. My eyes follow his hard features and I can't help but reach up and let the tips of my fingers trace the line of his jaw, feeling the . His eyes get even darker and his head leans down and his lips take mine, soft and slow. My fingers tangle in his hair and my other hand cups his jaw. As we kiss, that hand travels lower and I explore the contours of his body. Everything about him is so hard and I can feel the heat of his body radiating through his cotton shirt. His chest is so broad, the muscles contracting as my hand runs over them. His arms are what get me, so big and strong and I can feel the veins running down them. These are arms that I want to be held in, that I want to protect me. My hand reluctantly moves away from them to explore the other parts of his body. It travels down his torso, feeling every individual bump of his abs, and stop right above the waistline of his sweats."Sephie," His voice is dark, a warning for me to stop my exploration now, before he loses control. It's a warning I don't heed, my hand traveling over that bulge. He growls my name, hips thrusting into my hand. His reaction makes my stomach clench while at the same time making me feel like I'm on top of the world. Cool and collected Dominic is putty in hands as my finger wrap around him. I can feel every vein on his hardness and he throbs in my hand."My god, Sephie. I can't-" His words are cut of by a deep, rumbling groan when my hand strokes him. He quickly grabs my wrist, stopping my movements."Sephie, are you sure you want to do this," His chest rises and falls with his heavy breathes and his eyes look almost crazed with lust. "I want to make you feel good," I tell him honestly. I want to learn everything that makes his breath hitch and his hips thrust into my hand. I've never done anything like this but I completely trust Dominic to be gentle with me. His grip loosens on my wrist and this time my hand snakes beneath the waistline and onto his hot, bare flesh. He hisses at the skin to skin contact. He's so hard but at the same time, the skin is so soft. I can feel the pulse of his heartbeat and my finger trace over one of the veins. He feels so good in my hand but I need to see him with my own eyes. I pull his member out and it springs from the waistband of his sweats, so hard that it rest against his belly. "Fucking christ, Sephie," He growls. I admire him, so hard and veined, the tip red with need. My hand is back on him, stroking. I've never seen Dominic lose control like his. He curses and ruts up against me like a wild animal. What we're doing feels filthy, but the good kind of filthy, the kind that makes your heart race and cheeks flush. His lips crash against mine as I stroke him, this kiss urgent and filled with desire. Our teeth knock together and his groans fill my mouth. My hand moves over him faster and his lips are off of mine, a beautiful look of pleasure-pain crossing his features. He grows bigger in my hand, throbbing even more. I know he's almost there and my eyes travel from his face to his member. A drop of moisture has welled up at the tip and before I can even think, my mouth is on him, desperate for a taste. "Sephie! Fuck, I'm going to cum," He snarls. He pulses in my mouth and then his taste fills me. His hips thrust up, careful not to go too far and make me choke. The trusting slows and then comes to a complete stop. He pulls me up and lays me on the bed, lips immediately coming to my neck, hot kisses trailing down. Hit hot mouth covers the tip of my breast through my shirt and my back arches, unhuman sounds leaving my mouth. His hands trail up under my shirt and I shiver at his touch. He slowly lifts it until it's just under my breast and then he's kissing my stomach, my fingers clutching his hair. I want to cover my self up with my hands, feeling too naked and vulnerable. This is a place that I try my hardest to hide, especially from him, and now he's right there, hot kisses trailing over it. Then his mouth is traveling up, pushing the shirt up as he goes. He pulls it off and for the first time, eyes other than my own appraise me. He leans down and his mouth is covering my nipple, this time there's no shirt between us. I cry out at the sensation, hands pulling at his hair too hard. He goes between each breast, until I'm a hot puddle of need on the bed, shaking and begging. Finally, his mouth travels down, towards the place where I desperately need him. His lips reach the waistband of my sweats, his fingers going under and slowly pulling them down, along with my panties. I help him, lifting my hips off the bed and kicking them off. Now I'm completely naked, laid bare in front of this man who looks down at me like I'm the best thing he's ever seen, appraising every part of me, every flaw that I've desperately wished away like it's a work of art."Sephie, you are the most beautiful thing I have ever seen," He tells me and his voice thick with emotion as he looks down at me, my bare chest, flushed cheeks, and swollen lips. The way he says it makes me want to believe him, believe that everything I've thought about myself is wrong.His mouth is back on me then, more urgent than before, trailing down my stomach. His lips scorch their way down over my pelvis and my breathing intensifies, achingly waiting. His rough hands spread my thighs and my most private place is bare to his eyes."Fuck, Sephie," He growls, then his mouth is on me and my back is arching off the bed, mouth open in a silent scream. It's too much, the pleasure so intense it's almost painful. I try to pull away but his hands hold my thighs down, forcing me to take everything he gives me. His mouth works me over until I'm crazed with lust, filthy words I never thought I'd say leaving my mouth. This seems to urge him on and he's feasting on me like a starving man. I'm climbing higher and higher and then the world goes still as the unbelievable pleasure takes over and I tumble down, falling hard from the high. It seems to last forever as I writhe and moan, hands pulling at Dominic's hair. Then it's over, and I'm a sweaty mess on the bed."Jesus, Sephie, you're going to be the end of me," He tells me, taking my still shaking body into his arms. My head rests on his chest and we lay like that for a while, until our breathing slows. His hand slowly strokes my hair, and I'm so exhausted from all the intense emotions that just wracked my body that I find my eyes slowly closing on their own accord and soon I'm asleep in the safety of Dominic's arms.

Dominic really knows how to take care of Sephie...In more ways than one

If you like this chapter turn that little star down there orange (I feel like youtube every time I write this lol)

Chapter Eighteen

The smell of ham and sweet potato pie makes my mouth water as I help Dee and Judy set the table. Today is Christmas Eve and Silas and Mia came over for dinner before Dominic and Judy have to leave. Once everything is done, we all take our seats at the table, passing food around while talking.Dominic sits next to me, hand covering my thigh under the table, the touch sending tingles down my spine. The past few nights leading up to today we explored each other in the darkness of the room, totally absorbed in each other's bodies. By now, Dominic knew my body better than me. It's like he has an instruction manual on what made me tick."So, Sephie, how did it go down at the Bookshop today?" Judy asks, snapping me out of my inappropriate thoughts about her son."Oh-uh it was good. The gingerbread cookies were a hit, especially with Dominic" I respond, remember with amusement Dominic taking several home to save for later."That's good, Sephie. I'm glad you're making my boy happy," She tells me, reaching over to squeeze my hand, face softening in way that made my eyes sting a little. Sometimes I get a little jealous of Dominic that he has such a great mom.The rest of dinner is filled with happy chatter. This is the first real family dinner I've ever had and when we're done, I'm stuffed and happy at how the day turned out. Sadly, Judy's flight back home is tonight, she's spending Christmas day with the rest of their family back home. She pulls me into a tight hug before she leaves, and I wave in the driveway as they all leave, grateful for their company.I nervously go back in the house with Dominic. This is the first time we've been alone since his mom got here. It's perfect for what I have planned for today. I want to go all the way with Dominic tonight since this is his last night here before he leaves. I know we've only been dating for a little while but I trust Dominic with my whole body and heart. I may regret this later if Dominic decides he's bored with me and wants to break up, but that's too painful a thought and I want to focus on what I'm feeling now in the moment.The sound of Dominic's phone ringing brings me out of my thoughts. When he pulls the phone out and sees whatever is on the screen he lets out a curse."I have to take this, Sephie," He says, going into the bedroom. I awkwardly stand in the living room, knowing he wants privacy. I gaze around, surveying the little Christmas tree Judy insisted she buy for us and the presents beneath them. The other day I remembered that I hadn't gone Christmas shopping and made a frantic trip to the mall to get everyone something. Dominic reappears in the room, jaw tight and eyes hard. "There's been a change in plans. I have to leave tonight," He says."What happened?" I ask, disappointed. I was really looking forward to our last night together before he leaves."Tomorrow's flight got canceled. I have to leave tonight or else I won't be able to get there on time."Disappointed, I sit on the bed and watch as Dominic hurriedly packs his clothes in a duffle bag. In the back of my head, I'm slightly relieved that tonight is postponed. I was excited to be with Dominic tonight but it also is a little nerve-wracking.When he's done packing, I walk with him to the front door. I abruptly stop, remembering the Christmas present I got Dominic lying under the tree. I quickly get before heading back outside. There's a taxi out front waiting for him."Here," I say, handing hip the neatly wrapped dark blue box. I've never bought a guy a present before, so I had no idea what to get him. I settled on a beautiful pair of silver cuff links. "Thank you," Dominic took the box in his hands, eyes softening as he did."I want you to stay with your sister and Silas while I'm gone. The MC is still after you and you're not safe here alone," He says, eyes and voice still soft. "Okay, Dominic. I'll be there in the morning," I tell him. He leans down and presses his lips against mine for a short but sweet kiss. "I'll call you every day, okay?" He says. "Okay," I reply. I watch him leave down the driveway, wondering how I'll survive this week without him. When the taxi is gone, I go back inside, noticing how empty it feels in here. I send Mia a text, telling her that I have to stay at her house, before heading off to bed. Both Judy and Dominic had to leave before Christmas, which is a bummer. The guest room is free now, but I still choose to sleep in Dominic's room. Even though he's gone, his smell is still in the sheets, and I huddle up in them, wishing he was here. It feels strange falling asleep without my head on Dominic's chest or his arm around my waist. I toss and turn for hours, until falling into a restless slumber.

Chapter Nineteen

I sat on Silas and Mia's couch as we opened our presents. Early this morning I packed all the presents from under the tree in the car, along with a duffle bag full of clothes."Sephie! Thank you!" Mia squealed, pulling me into a tight hug when she saw the handbag I got her. I went back to opening the one from Leah and tears nearly welled up in my eyes from what was inside. There was a cookbook and with it a note that read:Sephie,

It was wonderful spending time with you. I can see the way my son lights up around you. My boy likes to eat, so hopefully, this will help you cook wonderful meals for him and possibly my future grandbabies.

-Judy"Aw, that's so sweet of her. You've only known them for a short amount of time but you already seem to be a part of the family," Mia says, looking over the note. Her words do make me a little nervous. Dominic and I seem to be moving at light speed, we've only been officially dating for a while and I'm already on good terms with his family.My present to both Silas and Mia was a reservation at one of the fancy restaurants in town. For the first time, the usually stoic Silas gave me a slight smile of gratitude. Mia gave me an E-reader, knowing that I love reading romance books. When I thought we were done opening gifts I noticed another present. I was surprised that on the box, there was a note saying 'To Sephie,

From Dominic'. I didn't notice him put anything under the tree or him even go out to buy anything.The wrapping paper is a beautiful lavender shade with a dark purple silk bow and it's small and rectangular. I almost feel bad ruining the paper by opening it. Inside lies a black jewelry box, the name of an expensive jewelry company engraved on it. Inside this, a beautifully delicate silver necklace with a gorgeous heart pendant encrusted with pink jewels."Whoa," I say, holding it up in my hand and admiring it. The reflects off the crystals beautifully."Wow, Sephie. I think it's fair to say you're getting under this guy's skin," Mia says, looking at the necklace in amazement. Her words send a girly giddiness through me and I actually let out a giggle. I feel like I'm in high school all over again, obsessing over some cute boy, except this time it's a man, a man who I've shared a bed with and did some R-rated r things in said bed."I'm so happy that you found someone who can bring that smile out of you. What did Dee and I tell you about opening your heart?" Mia says, an 'I told you so' look on her face. I want to believe her, I really do, but this all seems unreal. Girls like me don't get happy endings and macho men who care for them and protect them. In the back of my head, I'm trying to enjoy while it lasts, before I get my rude awakening***The next day, Mia and I roam around the mall. To my disappointment, Dominic hasn't called and my calls to him go unanswered. Instead of watching me mope around the house all day, Mia has decided to take us out for a girl's day. Silas is working and we're technically not supposed to be doing this since we have a motorcycle club on our behinds but Mia convinced me to take the risk.

We're walking in the food court when Mia abruptly stops, hand clutching her mouth."That smell makes me want to gag," She says, sounding sick. Confused, I sniff the air, only smelling the hot dogs from a fast food place near us."Do you need to sit down?" I ask worriedly."I think I'm going to be sick," She blurts out, running towards the nearest facilities. I rush after, only to find her puking in the toilet. One of the things that gross me out most in the world is the sound of someone puking, but I still hold her hair back and hold my breath, trying not to gag."Are you okay," I ask her when she's done. She gets up and rinses her mouth out in the sink before answering me."I don't know. That's been happening a lot lately. The smell of frying food makes me want to throw up. I get sick every morning," She tells me."Oh my god, you're not pregnant, are you?" I ask. I've watched enough T.V to know that those are classic symptoms of pregnancy."I can't be. I'm on the pill.""Are you taking it regularly?" I ask and her look of guilt gives me my answer."Oh my god, we have to get a pregnancy test kit," I tell her, pulling her hand and leading her out of the restroom."I don't think it's that serious. Maybe I'm just coming down with something. It is flu season," She tells me, but I ignore her, going into one of the mall's stores and heading towards the aisle with the kits. I pick up two, just in case, and on the way to the register, I get a large carton of orange juice. The older lady at the register gives a knowing look while ringing us up."Good luck," She says, handing us our receipts. Mia's face turns red and I lead her out of the store."Here, drink this," I tell her, handing over the orange juice. It takes a while for her to chug it down and when she's done we leave the mall, into the parking lot. The drive home is full of tension and Mia looks pretty nervous. When we pull up in her driveway she looks likes she's dreading this whole thing."It's going to be okay," I tell her, squeezing her hand. She gives me a slight smile and we leave the car and go into the house.I wait outside the bathroom door, pacing nervously. I jump when the door opens and she comes out."What did it say?" I ask."I don't know yet. I couldn't bring myself to read the results," Mia tells me. She looks so scared and I've never seen her that way. She's always been my big sister, the strongest one of the two of us but now she's the one needing my support. I pull her tightly into my arms and Mia hugs me back twice as hard."No matter what the results are, we'll figure this all out, okay?" I tell her. She nods her head in the crook of my neck and I reluctantly let her go.The two tests are sitting on the bathroom sink, facing down. I take a deep breath and close my eyes before picking them up and flipping them over in my hand. I say a quick prayer before I open my eyes to see the result.

Demon's Destiny just made it to 1k views! Thank you guys for reading!

Chapter Twenty

The two pink lines stared back at me on both of the tests. I don't know if I should be worried or happy, so I just stick to shocked. "What does it say," Mia asks anxiously from behind me. "They're both positive," I breath out, still staring at those two pink lines. "Oh my god. Ohmygod ohmygod ohmygod," Mia's high pitched said in quick succession. "What are you going to do?" I ask her, putting the tests down and facing her. "I'll be there for you one hundred percent of the way no matter what path you choose to take." "I think... I think I'm going to do it. I'm going to be a mom," She says in a low whisper. I yelp, pulling her up in my arms and spinning her around. "I'm going to be an aunty!" I scream loudly before putting her down. "Aunt Sephie," Mia says with a smile. "That reservation I gave you guys is for tomorrow night. You can break the news to Silas then," I tell her. "I don't know how he'll feel about this," Mia says nervously. "Silas loves you. I see the way he looks at you like you're his whole world. You have nothing to worry about," I reassure her, squeezing her hand. "Thank you, Sephie. I couldn't have asked for a better sister.***Dominic still hasn't called. I anxiously pick at my coffee cake, trying to rationalize it in my head. Maybe he's busy? Or he just needs space? But that insecurity lingers in the back of my mind. He could be tired of me and now that he's had time away from our relationship he realizes that he's out of my league. Or he met another girl, a girl who's slender and beautiful and experienced in bed. My stomach twists, the thought of Dominic with another woman too much to handle."You look anxious today," I jump in surprise at the sudden sound. Chris has walked over and sat next to me in the coffee nook without me even noticing."Sorry for startling you," He says."What do you want?" I ask, still a little mad at his actions from the fair. Most of the anger has worn off from our time apart but the wound still hurts."I want to apologize...If you'll let me," He says, with pleading eyes. "Fine, but that doesn't mean I'll forgive you," I tell him. Chris has been my friend for a long time and I miss our friendship. He was a big part of why I took the job at the bookshop. Working with him was fun and now that we aren't on good terms the only person I have talked to is Leah and the new girl who tried to hit on Dominic."Sephie, I really did like you but I just wasn't man enough to tell you. And it is true, I did want to wait until I was ready for a commitment to pursue you. Dominic was a rude awakening for me, that if I didn't make my move you would move on. I did it in the worst way possible and I lost a good friend in the process. Even though it still stings a little, I'm happy that you're with Dominic. I can tell he really cares about you. I know I really messed up but I don't want to lose your friendship."I soak in his words for a while, keeping quiet. He does sound genuinely sorry and he admitted that he messed up."I don't want to lose your friendship either. I hope things won't be awkward between us," I say, giving in."They won't! We'll pretend none of this ever happened," He says eagerly."I still don't trust you," I admit."I know and I'm going to do everything in my power to fix that."

Really short chapter today but I hoped you guys liked it. If you did, please leave a vote.

Chapter Twenty-One

It's the day of Dominic's fight and he still hasn't called me. By now I'm a total wreck, wondering what I did wrong. I stopped leaving messages days ago, not wanting to seem like an overbearing girlfriend. I know he's busy preparing for his fight but he can't set aside one minute to call? He promised he'd call every day and I can't help but feel betrayed that he broke that promise."Sephie! Stop moping! You're reading way to much into this," Mia says. We're in the waiting room of the hospital, waiting to be called for her first ultrasound. Silas is busy working again, which was pretty disappointing for Mia."What am I supposed to think. Everything was so good and he just stops talking to me out of nowhere? He's gotten bored of me.""I doubt anyone can get bored of you but if that's the case he's an idiot. I really doubt that's what's happening. He was so enraptured by you. A man doesn't feel that way about a woman and then ghosts her unless he's stupid. Just wait to hear his side of the story before you jump to conclusions, okay," Mia says giving me the big sister look."You're right. I am overthinking it a bit," I admit, calming down. This is going to be the biggest fight of his career and I know he's probably nervous right now."He'll be back soon. Just wait it out," Mia reassures me.The receptionist calls Mia's name and we follow a nurse with a clipboard into the ultrasound room."If you'll just lay down," The nurse says motioning towards the hospital bed.

"I'll give you girls a moment of privacy.""I'm so nervous," Mia says when the nurse leaves."It's going to be all right. You'll have a healthy baby," I reassure her."I know... I just wish Silas was here.""I'm sure he does too, Mia. Maybe you should talk to him about hiring more people to help with the business. He needs to be here more often for you and the baby," I tell her. I know Silas loves her but he has too many responsibilities with his business."You're right. There just are not that many people he trusts enough to help him with it," Mia sighs. We're both lost in thought until the doctor comes in a few minutes later."Sorry for the wait." She says. She's a middle-aged woman with dark skin kind brown eyes. We greet her and she begins the process of the ultrasound, rubbing the clear gel on Mia's not yet round stomach. She runs the device over it and I look intently at the on-screen monitor, trying to get my first look at my niece or nephew."Do you see that little blip on the screen?" The doctor says, motioning to what looks like a little peanut on the monitor."Oh my god! That's my baby," Mia says, tearing up. I grab and squeeze her hand, throat too thick with emotion to comfort her."There's the heartbeat," The nurse points to the small movement on the screen."Oh wow, it's so fast," I say fascinated."That's normal, babies hearts beat faster than our own. You look to be about one month along, Mia," The nurse says."You need to come back here in a month for another check-up. In the meantime, take your prenatal vitamins and avoid alcohol," She says sternly."I'll stay on top of it," Mia agreed.Afterward, Mia and I take the printed picture of the ultrasound and leave the clinic to prepare for the New Year's get together we're hosting.***Mia and Dee goofily danced around the house to oldies on the radio, having had one too many. Not being much of a dancer, I sat on the couch with Silas, watching with amusement. Leah and her wife Kristy were here, in the kitchen pouring themselves a glass of wine before the countdown started. Kristy bought her famous homemade cookies over, which I've eaten so many of I'm sure I'll have a stomach ache."It's about to start!" I announced seeing the beginnings of the countdown on the T.V."Do you want a glass of wine, Sephie?" Leah asked from the kitchen.

I politely declined. I've never been one to like alcohol, seeing what it did to my mother.Mia and Dee stop their dancing and sit on the couch, Mia on Silas's lap. Leah and Kristy also sat together on the loveseat. Seeing all the couples together is making me wish Dominic was here. His fight tonight has me worried, wondering if he's going to be alright. He would be entering the ring by now, and the thought sent a flurry of anxiety in my belly. The ball is ten seconds from dropping, and everyone counts down, Excitement feeling the room."Three, Two, One... Happy New Year!" Silas pulls mia in for a passionate kiss and Leah and Kristy clink their glasses together, lovingly looking into each other's eyes. I'm a little bummed, my boyfriend being a plane ride away and in possible danger."Happy New Year," I mutter to myself, picking up one of Kristy's famous cookies.After a while, I excuse myself to the restroom while they happily chatter about new year's resolutions and whatnot. I don't even have to use it, I just sit on the toilet, scrolling through the rows of texts I sent Dominic, hoping a message from him would pop up. I think wish has come true when my phone rings but to my disappointment, it's an unknown number. "Hello," I answer, wondering who would be calling me minutes after the new year struck."Sephie, It's your mother," Her raspy voice says from the other line. My mood worsened, wondering what trouble she wanted to bring my way."What do you want? I'm not going to steal from my boyfriend, so just leave me alone!" I snarled, my mood sour from her calling on top of the fact that I hadn't talked to Dominic in a week."Well, I just might have something that will change your mind.""What do you mean? Nothing will-" She hangs before I can finish and I stare at my phone in disbelief. Seconds later, a message appears on my phone from the same number.I click on and am surprised to see it is an image. It's blurry so I wait for it to fully load and when it does I feel my whole world crash down around me.Because right there on my phone was a picture Dominic, lips locked with a gorgeous brunette.

Chapter Twenty-Two

My heart breaks and tears flood my ears. You can't exactly make out his face all the way, but you can definitely tell it's him. Not many people have that big of a build and his dark hair and good looks. He's in red boxing shorts and sweat glistens on his skin. You can tell he just got through fighting. It doesn't escape me that the brunette is everything that I am not. Tall and slender, long sleek deep brown hair. She looked like she could grace the cover of magazines.

I wipe my tears and turn my phone off, slipping it back into my pocket, leaving the restroom.

"Are you okay, Sephie?" Mia asks, a worried look on her face.

"Stomach ache. Too many cookies," I reply dryly, wanting nothing more than to disappear and never be seen again.

"I told you my cookies were a hit. One bite and you can't put em' down," Kristy bragged. Usually, I would be amused by her humor but I just feel achingly numb. I sit down on the couch next to Silas and Mia and try my best to pretend the rest of the night.

Mia and Kristy drive off and we stand on the porch waving at them. I excuse myself to the guest room quickly, not wanting anyone to catch on to my mood. I strip off my clothes, not bothering to put them in the hamper, just leaving them on the floor. I get in the shower, purposely making the water way too hot. The burning takes my mind off of those images, the images that keep trying to repeat themselves in my head.

Before I realize it, my fingers are pruned and the bathroom is filled with steam. I get out, drying off and wrapping a towel around me. When I go back into the room. Mia is sitting on the bed.

"Sephie, what's going on?" She asks and I know that she sees right through my facade. I sit on the bed next to her, still wrapped in the towel, and let it all out.

"D-Dominic cheated on me. I was right all along, he's way out of my league. I was deluding myself thinking I can be with a guy like him," I explain, tears running down my cheek.

"Why do you think this? I'm sure Dominic would never do anything to hurt you," Mia says, looking apprehensive. I get my phone from my pants pocket and power it on. When it finally turns on I pull up the conversation, noticing that my mom sent me another message. I ignore it, opening the image and showing it to Mia.

"I-I...He wouldn't do that. I can't believe..." Mia stutters in disbelief.

"Don't deny. I was right about myself all along, Mia, wasn't I?" I ask, already knowing the answer. Dominic was never really attracted to me. I was just easy to access and clearly a fool. We weren't even together a month before I wanted to give him my virginity.

"I'm s-s-so stupid!" I cry, chest heaving with sobs. Mia pulls me into her chest.

"You're not stupid, you just have a big heart. There's nothing stupid about that. You can stay here when Dominic comes back, okay?" I nod my head against her chest, small sobs still racking my frame. When they finally stop, Sephie says her goodbyes and leaves me to my misery in the room.

I get up and blindly pull out an outfit from my duffle bag and put it on. I get in bed, not bothering to put my hair up knowing I'll pay for it in the morning. Even though I'm troubled I surprisingly find sleep easily. My dreams are plagued with the images of the nights Dominic and I spent in his room together except this time I'm replaced with the slender brunette woman.

***

Dominic's POV

For the first time in my life, I think I'm going to lose my fight.

Devil is relentless, throwing punch after punch to my ribs. I may be fast but he's just as fast and his hits are as powerful as mine. Never has there been a fight with such evenly matched people. We seem to get nowhere, going on match after match. I feel myself tiring, my body aching from all the hits I've taken and the adrenaline wearing off. I wonder if he's tired too but his face is a mask of determined fury, as I'm sure mine is.

Devil lays a powerful punch to my ribs and I swear I hear them crack. For the first time since I had my first fight in high school, I fall down.

"And Demon is down! For the first time in history, Demon has taken a fall!" The announcer yells. The crowd chants my name and the referee counts down the seconds. Just before he reaches one, I pull my self up, my ribs screaming in agony. Devil eyes me and I can tell he thinks he's going to win.

The referee calls for the next match to start and Devil and I circle each other. Devil throws the first punch, aiming for my ribs, the spot he knows is weak. I grit my teeth as he lands a punch on my already agonized ribs and I know I'm going to lose.

The image of Sephie appears in my head, her smile, her curls, her curves. I have to do this for her, I have to win. Devil aims for another punch to my ribs, leaving his face open for only a split second. That's enough for me and I take my chance, landing a furious punch on his temple, the force hurting my knuckles. Devil drops to the concrete floor, out cold.

"Three, two, one...Demon, once again, is undefeated!"

The crowd goes crazy, their screams so deafening that I hear my ears ring. Austin and his boys escort me out of the ring and several people have to have to hold the crowd back.

"I thought you were going to lose that one," Austin tells me sounding relieved. Me too, I think dryly.

"I fucking love you, Demon!" I hear a high pitched female voice say. I'm used to hearing comments like these put this is coming from way too close by.

I stop and turn around, seeing a skinny brunette girl who happened to make it through the crowd. Before I can call security over to get her, she runs up to me, wrapping her arms around my neck. She pulls me down to her and her dry, thin lips are on mine. My own lips curls in disgust, used to the feel of Sephie's soft plump ones. Somewhere in the distance, I catch the quick flash of a camera phone.

"Get the fuck off of me," I snarl, putting my hands on her shoulders and pushing her away from me. She stumbles back, cheeks reddening in embarrassment. Security quickly grabs her, dragging her out of the premises by the arm.

"Desperate groupies," I mutter, following after Austin.

***

My head pounds to the beat of the loud bass playing from the speakers. Once again I've been forced to attend one of these after-parties. I down the bitter liquid from the red solo cup, watch the grinding bodies around me. I don't want to be here, I want to be back home in bed with my Sephie. I haven't talked to her in a week and the distance is unbearable. Austin insisted I focus all my attention on training and went as far as taking my phone. I was angry at first but I realized it was for the better. I didn't need distractions. After this fight, I can retire and focus all my energy on me and Sephie. I know Sephie doesn't want to spend her life worried about me getting hurt in a fight. She deserves better and I'm going to give it to her.

"Fuck this shit," I mutter, leaving the red solo cup and making my way out of here. I'm going to book a flight home for tonight. I'm in no condition to fly after this fight but I don't care. I need to get back to my girl.

I make my way out of the rented mansion into the cold night air. I know Austin is going to lose his shit but I don't care, this is my last fight anyway.

"If it isn't Demon his self," I hear a voice say from behind me. I turn around, ready to defend myself but it's Devil, leaning against the wall.

"What do you want?" I ask suspiciously. Many times fighters have sought revenge after losing their undefeated title to me.

"I hold no grudge," Devil says, holding both hands up. I notice he sports a gruesome-looking knot on his temple. "In fact, I respect you. Any man who can beat me holds high regards in my book."

I give him a lift of the chin, still not knowing what his intentions are.

"I just need to know how you did it. I've been fighting since I was sixteen, never lost once. We were evenly matched and I got you pretty hard in the ribs. How could you have recovered from that?" He asks.

"When you have someone you care about counting on you, there's not much you can't do," I tell him truthfully.

"Your woman?" He asks. I nod.

"Maybe that's just what I need," He mutters, almost to himself. "Thanks for giving me the fight of my life, man. Haven't had a challenge like that in years, it's refreshing."

He returns into the party, the muted sound of pounding speakers loudening when he opens the door. I walk to my rented car, ready to go back to my hotel and find the quickest flight back home. My phone vibrates in my pocket before I start the car.

"Demon," I answer gruffly, wanting to get home.

"What the hell is wrong with you, man?" Silas growls loudly in my ear.

"What the fuck are you talking about. I don't have time for this, I need to get back to my woman."

"I doubt you're going to have a woman to get home to. Why the fuck am I looking at a picture of you locking lips with a groupie?"

"What?" I ask, my stomach dropping in surprise.

"You know what the fuck I'm talking about. Sephie's mom sent her the picture. Clue in on this: When Sephie's sad, her sister is sad. When Mia's sad, I'm pissed. If you want to fuck around, do it on somebody that's not my girl's sister."

"What the fuck," I growl. "That picture was taken out of context. Some groupie bitch kissed me and I told her to fuck off."

"Well, you need to let Sephie in on this. Mia is stressed and I don't take kindly to that considering she's carrying my baby."

"Shit, man," I mutter, not knowing Mia was pregnant.

"Shit indeed. Take the next flight down and fix this mess," He hangs up and I'm left in the car in silent fury.

"Fuck!" I snarl, slamming my fists against the steering wheel. I quickly get a move one, starting the car and head straight to the airport. If they don't have a flight for tonight I'll raise hell until they do.

I drive like a bat from hell, the whole time the thought of losing Sephie haunts me.

Chapter Twenty-Three

An incessant pounding in my head pulls me out of my sleep. I'm confused at first, opening my eyes and seeing morning light just coming through the window. The pounding goes on and on and when the fog of sleep clears from my head I realize I'm not just imagining it. Someone is pounding on the bedroom door.

Thinking it's an emergency and Mia needs me I quickly get up and unlock the door, pulling it open. Before I can see who it is they're pushing their way in my room and closing the door behind them. I don't even have to look up to know who it is. I smell the faint scent of the body wash he always uses.

"What are doing here?" I ask, trying my best to keep my voice void of emotion. We're both standing in the middle of the room and Dominic's large presence seems to fill the whole space.

"Sephie..." Dominic's hands find my side and slide down to my hips and he presses his forehead against mine. I want so badly to lean into him which confuses me. Why do I want to be close to someone who hurt me like this? This is too much. I push away from him, backing up until the back of my legs hit the edge of the bed.

"You don't get to touch me. You got what you wanted, didn't you? You got to have your fun and play with the stupid insecure girl's heart. You can go back to banging random groupies now," I can't help but let a tremble escape in my voice at the last sentence.

"Are you going to let me explain myself?" Dominic asks.

"There is nothing to explain. I saw the picture, Dominic."

"You saw how those girls were at the fights. They're crazy. Some groupie walked up to me and kissed me. Before I could tell her to fuck off someone took the picture," I feel hope welling up in my chest but I quickly force it down, not wanting to get hurt again.

"It's not suspicious to you how your mom got ahold of the picture? Right after wanting you to steal fifty grand from me? She's trying to break us up."

I can't help but think he has a point. My mom had to be the one to take the picture or least get the picture from someone else and she's not exactly the most reliable source.

"Why should I believe you?" I ask, the image of him and that girl still burned in my head. "Even if you are telling the truth, I can't do this. Wondering if you're going to choose someone else over me, questioning if I'll ever be good enough. It all just too much."

My voice breaks at the end and he pulls me into his arms. I can't stop myself from sinking into his touch this time, burying my face in his chest and letting it all out. Every doubt and every insecurity, I let it all out into him, ugly crying into his chest. Dominic picks me up and sits on the bed with, cradling me like a baby while I heave with sobs.

"When I said I was going to make you see yourself the way I do, I wasn't lying. I'm not going to give up on you, Sephie. I've only known you for so long, but you've already stolen my heart." It takes a while for my sobs to die down and Dominic strokes my hair, telling me how beautiful I am.

"I'm going to take you home now," Dominic tells. He picks up my duffle bag, and grabs my arm and pulls me off of the bed. I don't know how to feel about any of this so I don't protest, I just let Dominic lead me out of the room. Mia is in the kitchen, leaning against the counter when we get there. She says no words, looking between with a knowing look. Dominic leads me outside and opens the door for me and I get in the car, feeling numb and confused.

The ride to Dominic's house is short and before I know it we're pulling up in his driveway. He gets my duffle bag, comes around to open the door for me and leads me inside. We get into the bedroom and he sits me down on the bed.

"I have to take a quick shower. I'll be right back," He says, leaving to the restroom. While he's gone I sit on the bed, thinking about our relationship. I have a feeling he was telling the truth but I don't want to have to keep second-guessing myself. I don't think I can be with someone like Dominic without constantly questioning his feeling for me.

Dominic leaves the restroom, towel around his waist. I don't even try to avert my eyes when he drops his towel in front of the dresser. I gasp at the dark bruises littering his torso, mostly on his ribs.

"What happened?" I ask and can't help but reach out and run my finger softly over the scattering of blue and purple.

"The fight. It did a number on me," Dominic says.

"Did you win?"

"Yeah, I did. I would have lost if I didn't know I had you to come home to," I blush at his words, taking my hand away. Dominic pulls on a t-shirt and blue jeans before sitting next to me on the bed.

"I know your questioning things right now and I want you to know whatever you're thinking is wrong. I'm going to order some takeout for us and give you some space to think about everything," With that Dominic leaves and I'm left on the bed, wondering about the future of our relationship.

Chapter Twenty-Four

- -

For the first time, I wake up and Dominic is still asleep. His chest moves up down with his breathing under my cheek and his arm is wrapped around my back. I lift my head and my heart stops at his face. Dominic looks so cute while sleeping, dark eyelashes brushing his cheek, mouth slightly open, snore coming out. A five o'clock shadow has formed on his chin and I mindlessly lift my hands, brushing over the scratchy hairs. His eyes slowly open, blinking at first.

"Good morning," He says in his husky sleep voice.

"Goodmorning," I say back, blushing at being caught admiring him. I know I shouldn't have been doing that. For the past couple of days, things between Dominic and I have been tense. I don't know if I want to stay with him at the risk of being hurt. Just the thought of losing Dominic is too painful to bear so I know I should cut my losses before we get any closer.

"I just realized I haven't taken you out on a proper date," He tells me suddenly.

"What?" I ask in surprise.

"A date. The closest thing we had was the movies and that doesn't count. I'm taking you out tonight, Sephie."

"I don't think-"

"Good. Don't think," He says cutting me off. "I have things to do today, so you might want to stay with your sister. I'll be back around seven to take you to dinner," Before I can protest he gets up, going into the bathroom. I hear water running and sigh. So much for keeping my distance.

***

Mia and I browse the clothing racks and ever so often she pulls something totally unreasonable out and forces me to try it on. My date with Dominic was only hours away when I realized I didn't have anything to wear. Mia noticed me freaking out dragged me to the mall.

"Try this on. The color complements your skin tone," Mia says, holding the Scarlette fabric up to me. I reluctantly take the dress into the dressing room, knowing such a red shade isn't for girls like me. Red is a beautiful, sensual color. I should stick to black, which doesn't make me stand out plus it makes you look slimmer.

I strip my clothes and slide into the soft fabric, which feels good against my skin. I'm surprised when I appraise myself in the mirror. The dress hugs my curves but not in a clingy way that makes me uncomfortable. It's long-sleeved but the neckline exposes just a bit of cleavage and clings to my breast in an attractive way. At my waist, the skirt flares out, making my hips look curvier. It stops a couple of inches above the knee, a bit out of my comfort zone. Surprisingly, the scarlet does compliment my skin's pink undertone. I walk out of the dressing room and give Mia a little twirl.

"This is it. This is the dress! You look beautiful," Mia says, pulling me into her arms.

"I don't know. It's a little too much," I tell her.

"Bullcrap! Dominic is going to lose his mind when he sees you," Mia tells me.

"I'll get it," I give in, knowing she won't give up. Mia drags me over to the checkout line, still with dress on.

"I have to take it off first, Mia," I tell her, rolling my eyes.

"This is an emergency situation. Your date is in less than two hours and by the time you get home, Dominic will be waiting for you. You understand, right?" Mia says, directing the last question to the cashier.

"I don't care," The teenage girl says, looking bored. She rings me up and I pay for the dress.

Mia drags me around the mall, store to store. We buy a pair of black strappy pumps to compliment my outfit and at one of the makeup stores, we pay one of the workers to 'beat my face' as Mia calls it. In the end, I have a soft romantic makeup look and red lipstick paints my lips to compliment my dress. Finally, I get my hair straightened for the first time since prom. It reaches mid-shoulder, falling in soft romantic waves. By the time we walk out to the car, Mia is carrying a plastic bag with my old clothes in it and I'm getting stares on the way out. I can't help but notice that these are looks of admiration, which blows my mind.

Mia throws my clothes into the backseat, and we get in the car, driving straight to Dominic's house. When we pull into the driveway, I feel my palms sweat at Dominic car which is already there.

"It's going to be okay Sephie. Dominic is going to lose his mind when he sees you," Mia says, grabbing my hand reassuringly.

"I don't know. This whole opening my heart thing hasn't been working out for me," I tell her.

"I never said it would be easy, just worth it. You're going to look back on this and thank me one day," Mia tells me, squeezing my hand before I leave the car. I walk up the steps, heart drumming in my chest. Before my hand reaches the doorknob, Dominic opens the door making me jump.

"Jesus Christ, Sephie," Dominic says. His reaction is close to what Mia said it would be. His jaw drops and he looks at me in what can only be described as a mixture of admiration and lust. I blush at stare, probably looking the same way at him. For the first time, I see Dominic in a suit and I am not disappointed. The suit is charcoal black with a grey dress shirt and I notice the silver cuff links I gave him for Christmas. The suit makes his presence seem more dominating than it already is.

"You look beautiful, Sephie. Absolute perfection," He tells me.

"Thank you. You don't look bad yourself," I compliment him, blushing.

"Shall we," He says with a grin, holding his arm out to me. I take his offered arm and we leave the porch, heading towards his car.

"I told you he would freak, Sephie!" Mia yells from her car window, still in the driveway. Dominic chuckles and I blush as she drives away.

Dominic opens the car door for me and comes back around to get in. The ride is silent but comfortable, soft music playing from the radio. The drive is a long one, taking us out of the city. We don't arrive at our destination until eight-thirty. It's a fancy restaurant, one that you need a reservation for weeks ahead just to get into.

"Dominic, this place must cost a fortune, we don't have to go here," I tell him.

"You're worth a fortune, Sephie," With that he gets out and comes around to open the door for me.

Dominic keeps his hand on the small of my back as we walk into the restaurant. We're immediately greeted by the host and taken to our table, which is a little isolated from the rest of the packed restaurant. We're given our menus and left to ourselves.

"You've never told me about your upbringing, other than what I've already gathered from the situation with your mom," Dominic says.

"It's not that interesting," I tell him but he waits for me to continue.

"Well, my sister is older than me so she remembers my dad a little more than I do. From I can recall, he was always working and in a bad mood, except for when he was around my mom. He left when I was six to be with some other woman and mom went downhill from there. Mia was left to look after me a lot with mom drinking and gambling most of the time. She brought home a lot of boyfriends, and all of them were creeps. A few of them tried to harm me and my sister but Mia and I always had each other's back. Mia moved out to go to beauty school two years ago and met Silas and we drifted apart until I needed her help after the break-in,"

"I'm sorry that you went through that," Dominic says, reaching across the table and squeezing my hand.

"It's fine, that's all in the past. What about you, Dominic. I don't know about your past either." I ask. Before he can answer, we're interrupted by the waitress coming over to take our orders.

"Well," Dominic begins when the waitress leaves. "My family and I grew up in a pretty rough neighborhood. We never had enough food, the utilities got cut off a lot. My dad was...very abusive to my mom. A lot of the time she would be too hurt to take care of my sister so I had to help out a lot. When I got older I was able to defend my mom against my dad. When I was fifteen I kicked him out of the house. I started fighting to get enough money to pay bills around the house. I was really good at and now I'm able to support my family."

"Dominic..." I whisper, at a loss for words. The thought of anyone hurting sweet little Judy is too much to bear.

"That was a long time ago and everything's better now," Dominic tells me. The waitress comes over and gives us our food and from then on the conversation is light and humorous. We seem to talk for hours, caught up in our own little world. Before long our plates are empty and Dominic is paying the bill and walking me out to the car.

The ride is quiet and comfortable, and I stare out the window at the night view. I know I'm falling for Dominic, in fact, I think I've already fallen. It's scary to think but at this point, I can't imagine being without Dominic. I'm in love with him. Helplessly in love him. The thought is terrifying. I know it's too late to end this because I'm already emotionally invested. I should've run when I had the chance before he had the power to break my heart.

"Sephie," I jump at his soft voice in the quiet car. We are in his driveway, already home. I was lost in thought the whole way here.

"Thank you for tonight, Dominic. It was amazing," I tell him with a smile.

" I enjoyed it too. It won't be the last," He tells me. I reach over to unlock my door but he stops me.

"Sephie, wait," He says. "I just- I've never felt this way about anyone before. I've fallen for you, Sephie, and I fell a long time."

"Dominic..." I say, voice thick with emotion. I don't know what to feel or what to say. A part of me still doesn't want to believe him, even though he's laid it all out.

" I know you don't believe me but I'll wait however long it takes to convince you, Sephie."

With that, he leaves sitting in the car with these confusing thoughts and emotions.

Chapter Twenty-Five

S ix months later

"Isn't this just so adorable," Mia says, holding up the small pink tutu. She's really starting to show now, her rounded belly poking out from her cardigan. Mia, Dee, and I are shopping for baby clothes and things to decorate the nursery with. We found out Mia was having a baby girl two months ago.

"Look at this!" Dee calls from the other side of the store. We go over to her and she's pointing to one of the giant teddy bears on the store shelves.

"We have to get it! It's perfect for her room," Mia says, going to get a worker to get it from the shelf.

We walk out of the store with the giant teddy bear in tow, earning us a bunch of stares. It takes all three of us to squish it into the car and I feel bad for Dee, who has to squeeze in next to the giant thing.

When we get to Mia's house Silas is still busy with work. I know Mia's stressed out about having to be alone a lot so I've been trying to come over more. Dee and I go to the guest room, which now looks completely different, with a crib, changing table, and the walls half painted a baby pink, almost white color. Mia's too far along in her pregnancy for it to be safe to be around paint fumes so Dee and I are helping her. Dee turns on the radio and we concentrate on rolling the paint onto the walls.

"Is that Dominic's car?" Dee says later on, looking over at the window. I excitedly get off of the small later and go over to the window. Dominic and have gotten really close over these last few months. We nearly inseparable, spending every moment of our free time together. Just the thought of him makes my stomach flutter.

My brows crease in confusion when I look out the window. Dominic's car is a new model, sleek and grey. This one's also a new model but it's a van, black with darkly tinted windows. And it's just lingering outside by the curb, not even pulled into the driveway.

"That's not Dominic's car," I say, turning towards Dee.

"I thought so. It's just sitting there. That's so weird. We should call Dominic," Dee says, pulling out her phone. I shake my head, not wanting to bother him over something minor like this.

"It's fine. It'll probably just pull off any-" The words die in the mouth when the window explodes next to me, sending glass flying where. I scream, falling to the ground, glass painfully digging into my knees and hands. Loud popping sounds continue to go off and I realize that someone is shooting, most likely the person in the black car.

Bullets continue to fly through the room and I try to get far away from the window, but the glass is painfully digging into me. Dee grabs my arm and we scurry out of the room, crawling on the glass littered floor.

"Oh my god! What happened?!" Mia yells, helping me off of the ground.

"Someone just fucking shot at us! In the nursery!" Dee snarls, infuriated.

"I'm calling the cops," Mia says, pulling out her phone. Dee also gets out her phone to call Dominic. Now that some of the adrenaline has worn off, I notice my injuries. I have a bunch of cuts on my knees and hands, most of them shallow, but a few of them are deep, looking like they need stitches. I notice a burning sensation on my hip. When I touch it, my hand comes away with a surprising amount of blood.

"Oh my god, Sephie's bleeding!" Dee shouts, noticing the deep red coating my finger. I can almost hear Dominic freaking out on the other line.

"Nothing major got hit. I think it's just a flesh wound," I say, trying to calm myself. I go into the kitchen to get a towel. I press it against the wound and flinch at the shooting pain. I've always been a wuss when it comes to blood and pain and now that the adrenaline has I feel myself panicking.

I hear the blaring sirens outside when the police and ambulance arrive. Mia is the one to let them in and explain the situation to them. Dee is still on the phone with Dominic when one of the medics come up to me and checks my wound.

For the first time in my life, I'm put in the back of an ambulance on a stretcher. At this point, all of my wounds are throbbing in pain and I have to lean a certain way in order to keep pressure off of my hip. Dee and Mia are right behind us when we arrive at the hospital. I want to tell them I'm okay to walk but I keep my mouth shut as they lead me into the hospital room. A doctor is there waiting for me and I feel fear bubble up in my chest. I have a strong fear of needles and sharp things. I'm given a hospital gown and I change into it, wincing when I pull my pants down over my wounds.

"You have two wounds that need stitches on your knees. It looks like the bullet just grazed your hip but it's still a deep wound. I'll get you stitched up and prescribe you some antibiotics and pain meds," The doctor says after thoroughly examining me. I wince as she pulls out a long needle to numb the area, I clutch at the bed cloth beneath me, heart racing in my chest. I see movement near the entrance of the room and look up. My fears melt away when I see Dominic entering the room.

"Sephie, I was so worried," He says, sitting next to the bed and grabbing my hand.

"I'm just glad you're here right now," I tell him. His presence always makes everything better.

"Mia and Dee are being questioned right now. We're going to end all this mess," Dominic says, eyes set in fierce determination.

The doctor clears her throat, putting an end to our exchange. I look away as she numbs my wound, squeezing Dominic's hand whenever it hurts. After everything is numbed the procedure goes smoothly, I only wince a couple of times and Dominic is there to whisper an encouragement or squeeze my hand.

When everything is done, I'm given my prescription and orders to get a lot of rest and not overexert myself. Dominic and I leave the hospital room hand in hand to get my prescriptions.

Five chapters uploaded today! I'm on a roll!

I hope you guys liked this update! Please vote if you did!

Chapter Twenty-Six

Dominic's POV

I get out of bed and Sephie sleeping form rolls over to fill the space I was just in. The pain meds put her to sleep fast, which is good because I've been barely controlling myself while she was awake. Fury has been building under my skin since I first got the news that this someone shot at and hit my Sephie. The fact that this MC has the balls to do this is beyond me. They're are getting even more determined to make Sephie pay for her mother's debt and It's time they are dealt with.

When I get into the kitchen Silas is already there, leaning against the counter, a look dark as mine on his face.

"They've started a full-blown war now," Silas says, voicing my thoughts.

"They must have found out that Sephie's mom burned through all their money."

"They're getting desperate. They can't find her so they're turning all their attention on Sephie," Silas says to me.

"So what are we going to do about it. I'm ready to go down there right now," I tell him.

"Me too but we have to be patient. There are two hundred members and we don't have that manpower. We're going to have to hit them where it hurts."

"Moses," I say, already knowing I'm right. Moses is the leader of the mc and the one behind all of this. He was the one Sephie's mom stole from.

"Once he's out of the picture we make it known that anyone who fucks with Sephie fucks with us," Silas says. By us he didn't just mean him and I. We had a lot of people who would ride for us. One of Moses's rivaling MC leaders owes Silas a favor for doing a fight for him back in the day and his club is much bigger than Moses's.

"I call dibs on Moses," I tell him. I want him to suffer for everything he put Sephie through. Silas doesn't protest, knowing that my girl just got shot and I have a more personal issue with him.

When I return to our room I slide back into the bed with Sephie. Like always, she curls into my side, head resting on my chest. My arm snakes around her waist and I savor the moment. After worrying about her so much today it feels good to know she's safe right here with me.

I know this is a really short chapter but more is coming up soon!

Chapter Twenty-Seven

A /N: This chapter contains explicit sexual content.

Sephie's POV

Dominic walks me out of the movie theater, hand on the small of my back. Dominic didn't lie, there was much more to come after our first date. It seems like we go to a new place every week.

Since the shooting incident, I haven't been allowed to be out of Dominic's sight for anything other than bathroom breaks. The way he hovers over me is pretty hilarious if not cute and protective. Even though my wounds have mostly healed Dominic acts still like I'm a fragile piece of glass.

After Dominic opens my door for me I stare out the window on our way home, radio playing softly in the background. As usual, Dominic and I don't need to make conversation to fill the silence in the car. If I were around anyone else this would be awkward but because it's Dominic, I feel completely at ease.

Dominic comes around to open my door once we get home and his hand is on the small of my back, walking me into the house. When we reach the bedroom, I sit on the bed and Dominic sheds his clothes. Like aways,

I shyly avert my eyes even though I've already seen everything he has. He leaves into the bathroom and I hear the spray of water start.

That's when the nerves kick in. Before Dominic left for his fight, I said I was ready to give myself to him but the picture my mom sent me put a stop on all the progress I made on my confidence in my relationship with him. Now I know the picture was taken out of context. Deep down I know Dominic wouldn't do that to me. He's been nothing but caring and patient with me even though all my hang-ups. And now I know I'm ready, even more ready than I was before.

So, swallowing the lump in my throat, I shed my clothes before entering the bathroom. It's full steam and the smell of my his body wash fills the room. Before I open the shower door, I take a deep breath, bracing my self.

"Sephie..." Dominic's questioning voice trails off when he turns around and takes me in. I'm in nothing but my birthday suit and this time there we are not in the darkness of his room. The room is fully lit and he can see all of me, every flaw and every curve.

"Jesus, Sephie, you're beautiful," Dominic says, a look of awe on his face as he takes me in. Every inch of my skin warms as his eyes run over me. For the first time ever, I feel beautiful under his appraising gaze.

"Thank you," I tell him, shy under his eyes. He fills his hand with his body wash and reaches out to me. Everything in me tenses at the contact. His touch feels different with my skin slick with water and soap, like its igniting all the nerve endings in my body. My breath deepens as he runs the soap into my skin, no part of my body left untouched. When he reaches a particularly sensitive area breath catches.

When It's my turn I take my time, trying to memorize every inch of his body. Dominic's lean muscles feel amazing under my hands and a couple of times I hear a groan escape him. The growing pole between his legs doesn't go unnoticed by me. He curses when I take him into my hand and stroke him, the soap making everything feel slicker.

"Fuckin' hell, Sephie," He moans out. He slips out of my hand when his lifts me up, legs around his waist, and kisses me. The kiss is desperate and hungry, my hands threading through his hair and pulling hard.

I vaguely notice him moving him us from the steamy shower. I feel cold marble under my butt and I realize that he sat me down on the bathroom sink. His mouth is still taking mine, rough and desperate. Then his mouth is gone and he's turning me around, pulling me to him my back to his front. We are standing in front of a mirror and my eyes meet his lust-filled ones in the reflection. Mine drift closed and my head leans back and rests against his shoulder as his hand drifts between my legs.

"Look," He orders, hand working wonders on me. I obey him, forcing my heavy lids to open.

The erotic sight in the mirror makes me gasp. My eyes are hooded with lust and my lips are swollen from our kiss. I didn't even notice my hips were grinding against his hand until I saw it for myself. Dominic's dark eyes are on me, taking this all in. His other hand snakes around and comes up to my breast. My back arches against his torso as he takes my nipple between his fingers and I try to keep my eyes from drifting closed again.

"Do you see it, Sephie. This is how I see you," Dominic whispers roughly, breath fanning over the top of my head. I look and this time I take every-thing in, trying to see myself through his eyes. And I see it, the way my curls frame my face, my plump lips, the curve of my stomach and hips. Now that my eyes aren't searching for a flaw or something to criticize, I can see a little of what Dominic sees. We even look suited for each other, my curves contrasting perfectly with Dominic's hard muscles.

"I see it," I breathe out in amazement.

"You're beautiful, Sephie. Every inch of you."

I watch us in the mirror as Dominic's hand pleasures me, the erotic sight turning me on further. He takes me higher and higher and soon I'm crashing down, calling out his name. He turns me around and his mouth is on mine, this kiss more gentle than the one before.

Dominic pushes me back out of the bathroom until the back of my legs touch the bed and lays me down. He leans over me, kisses trailing down my neck, making me shiver. I gasp and arch my back as he kisses a particularly sensitive area. My breathing is coming out in gasps, my hands threading through his hair. When his head leans down to take my nipple in my mouth, my back arches.

"I need you, Dominic. Now," I gasp, desperate for him.

"Patience," He chides me, his attention back on my breast. I want to cry out in frustration as he teases me, making me feel like I'm coming apart at the seams. Finally, his lips come up to mine and he positions himself between my legs.

"Dominic..." I breathe when I feel him press against me.

"Are you sure," Dominic asks, cupping my face in his hands.

"Yes. I need you, Dominic," I tell him. He reaches down and positions himself at my entrance and I gasp at the sensation of him there. He pushes in slowly and after a while, I feel a burning discomfort. He notices my furrowed brow and stops for a second, waiting until I'm comfortable. When I'm no longer tense, he pushes all the way in.

I clutch at the sheets underneath me at the unfamiliar sensation. There is a slight discomfort with a too-full sensation, but also an underlining pleasure of having Dominic inside me. I feel completely possessed by him, he's all around me and inside of me.

"I'm going to move now," Dominic tells me when I relax again. He pulls out just a little and pushes back in sharply. My back arches and I cry out at the sensation.

"I'm okay. Keep going," I tell him, chest rising and falling with my heavy breathes. He begins a rhythm, pulling out and pushing back in slowly. The uncomfortable feeling is gone and I feel sharp pleasure whenever he pushes back in. I notice Dominic's breathing increase and he lets out a few groans. His pace speeds up and I'm letting uncontrollable cries of pleasure out. The faster he moves the more pleasure builds up. Just when I think I've reached the precipice, Dominic reaches down and rubs my clit. My hands go up to his shoulder and my fingernails dig in as come to pieces around him. I cry out his name as his thrusts get faster and uneven and then Dominic is there with me.

Dominics thrust slow down and then come to a complete stop. Both of our breathing is heavy and Dominic rests his forehead against mine.

"I love you, Sephie."

Everything in the world seems to stop at his words. My whole body tenses and I forget how to breathe. I love you, Sephie. Those words repeat themselves in my head like a broken mixtape and I analyze them in my head, trying to find a secret meaning. Something other than the unbelievable concept of Dominic Hayes being in love with me.

"I- you don't have to...People say a lot of things when they-"

"I'm not just saying it," Dominic says, cutting off my rambling. "I'm in love you. I've been in love with you for a while now. You mean everything to me, Sephie. I don't know who I would be without you. You complete me."

"Dominic," I say, my voice thick with emotion. "I love you too. I couldn't see why you wanted to be with me before but now I see. We were made for each other. You bring the best out of me and in turn, I bring the best out of you."

Dominic leans down and his lips graze mine softly.

"You're my forever, Sephie."

They dropped the L-bomb! And Sephie's finally starting to become more confident in herself!

If you liked this chapter, please leave a vote!

Chapter Twenty-Eight

One month later

It's about one o'clock in the morning when I wake to the phone ringing. Dominic groans into the top of my head, rolling over to get the phone from the nightstand.

"Who is it," He growls in his sleep husky voice. I want to scold him for being so rude but I'm too busy huddling into the warmth of the blanket and trying to find sleep again.

"What? This early," His worried voice pulls me out of my sleepy haze and I sit up, trying to hear their conversation.

"Sephie and I will be there right away," Dominic says, hanging up.

"What's going on," I ask, a dozen different scenarios running through my head.

"Mia's going into labor," He tells me. My heart drops to the pit of my stomach. Mia is one month away from her due date meaning that the baby is coming prematurely.

I'm out of the bed and blindly throwing on clothes and so is Dominic. I slide on a pair of shoes and put my hair in a bun as Dominic and I rush out of the door. A million worries rush through my mind as I get into the car.

"Everything is going to be alright, Sephie. Dee was born two months premature and she turned out just fine," His words do bring me a little comfort but I still worry the whole drive to the hospital.

When we arrive we both are out the door quickly, head towards the entrance and to the receptionist.

"We're here for my sister, Mia Marie McKay. She just went into labor," I hurriedly tell the receptionist. She gives us a room number and Dominic and I rush to the elevator. When we get to her floor we both are nearly sprinting as we look for her room number. We find it and rush in to see Mia laying on the hospital bed and Silas sitting next to her, his hand holding hers.

"Mia! Are you okay?" I ask, rushing to her side. Curls escape her messy ponytail and stick to the perspiration on her forehead and dark bags are under her eyes.

"I'm fine," She says, giving me a weak smile. "I've been in labor for a couple of hours. I thought I was just having Braxton Hicks until they kept getting more intense. I get a contraction every twenty minutes or so."

"I can't believe you're going to be a mom today," I say, tearing up a bit.

"Me either. It seems like just yesterday we gossiping about all the high school boys in our room," Mia tells me. I bend down and pull her slender frame into a hug.

Dominic and I take a seat at Mia's bedside as she goes through her contractions. It's so hard to see Mia in pain but I'm sure Silas is taking it harder than I am. He paces the room anxiously, hand running through his hair in frustration. Whenever Mia has a contraction, he's at her side, holding her hand and whispering encouragements to her. I can't help but be happy that Mia has a guy like Silas in her life.

***

It's early morning when the doctor who checks on Mia says she is fully dilated. Only one person is allowed to be present during the birth so Dominic and I are ushered out of the room. I sit in the waiting room, worrying about any complications happening during birth. Dominic reassures me a couple of times, squeezing my hand.

My relief comes when the doctor comes into the waiting room, a smile on his face.

"Your niece is ready to see you, Ms. Mckay."

I jump up from my chair and head into the hospital room. Mia is holding a cute little bundle with Silas at her side, looking exhausted but glowing like a proud momma.

"She's so beautiful. I'm so proud of you," I say, tears welling up in my eyes.

"She is. Here, hold her," She says, putting the little bundle in my arms.

I look down at my sleeping niece in amazement. Soft dark brown curls frame her head and she has a little button nose just like Mia and me.

"What's her name," I ask after I'm done cooing at her.

"Mila," Mia tells me.

"That's so beautiful," I put the little Mila back in her mother's arms.

Over the course of the day, a lot of people come over to visit Mia and her baby. By the time afternoon hits, Mila is spoiled and exhausted, having been held and cooed at by at least a dozen people. I'm exhausted from having my sleep interrupted and my stomach is upset from not eating the whole day. I tell Dominic that I'm going to get some food and excuse myself from the room.

As I'm walking I get light-headed. I want to blame it on the lack of sleep and hunger, but I've been feeling this way for the past week. Before I reach the hospital cafeteria, I start feeling faint. Instead of going in, I take a turn to the doors leading outside for some fresh air.

I lean against the hospital walls, trying to calm my nauseous stomach and spinning head. I close my eyes, savoring the fresh air after being stuck in the stuffy hospital room.

"Finally alone now, Sephie," I jump at the deep voice, eyes snapping open. Standing in front of me is the same man who broke into my trailer, all those months ago. My blood runs cold, looking for an escape. He's blocking the door and I know if I run he'll catch me.

"Dominic and Silas know I'm down here. You won't get away with anything, so just leave me alone," To my surprise, I successfully keep the tremble out of my voice.

"We both know that's not going to happen. You owe me and I'm not too happy about the stunt you pulled last time I tried to collect my debt. This time you'll cooperate or you may not come back to your little boyfriend in one piece."

As soon as the words leave his mouth I know he's intent on taking me. The only chance I have is to distract him so I can run back into the hospital and call for help. Before I can talk myself out of it, I feign a look of defeat on my face and walk towards him.

"That's what I thought. Little Sephie isn't as brave as she pretends to-" His words are cut off by a groan of agony when my knee comes up between his legs with all my strength. Before he can get his bearings, I run past him into the hospital.

"Help! Somebody's trying to kidnap me!" My scream is loud, echoing off the hospital walls. I know someone has to hear me and I continue to run, trying to make it to the cafeteria. Before I get there, a hard body slams into me, throwing me to the floor.

"You are going to get it now, bitch," He snarls above me. He grabs me and drags me out and I fight the whole way, scratching and punching at him.

"Hey! What do you think you're doing!" One of the nurses is there, my screams having caught her attention. I feel cold metal press into the side of my head and I tense, my whole body going cold.

"If I were you I would mind my business," He says coldly to her. Her face pales, and she pulls out her phone to call the cops. He continues to drag me out of the hospital, gun still pressed against my skull. I cooperate when he pushes me into a car, the same one that shot at us in Mia's nursery.

"I told you to fucking cooperate," He snarls at me. Before I can get my bearings, he slams the barrel of the gun into my temple. Intense pain radiates from the wound, and my world goes black, my last thought Dominic and the look on his face when he finds out that I'm gone.

Chapter Twenty-Nine

Trigger Warning: There is a scene with attempted sexual assault near the end of this chapter. Please skip ahead if anyone is triggered by this.

Dominic's POV

I anxiously pace the room, waiting for Sephie to come back from the cafeteria. She's been gone way too long, almost ten minuted. The cafeteria isn't far from here and it doesn't take that long to get food.

"I'm gonna go look for, Sephie," I tell Silas, who's sitting next to mia, holding his baby girl in his arms.

"She hasn't been gone that long. Maybe she had to use the bathroom," Mia says, rolling her eyes at me. I ignore her, heading out of the door. I have a bad feeling in the pit of my stomach as I make my way to the cafeteria. When I turn into the hallway where the cafeteria is, I see a nurse frantically talking into her phone.

"...He tackled her and threatened us with a gun. I saw him hit her with the gun in the parking lot. Please send a cop here immediately!" She frantically talks into the phone. My heart grows cold with fear and I rush into the cafeteria, hoping the nurse is talking about someone else. When I don't see her in there I go back into the hallway to talk to the nurse.

"The girl you're talking about- I think she's my girlfriend. Was she about 5'2, curly hair, wearing leggings and a grey hoodie?"

"Yes! That's her! Some guy just drove off with her seconds ago," The nurse tells me.

"Fuck!" I growl out through clenched teeth. A million thoughts race through my head about Sephie. Is she hurt? Am I going to get to her in time?

"Which way did they go?" I ask the nurse.

"They went down that way," She says, pointing to the right. "You should just let the police handle this." I ignore her advice, pulling out my phone and calling Silas as I head into the parking lot.

"They fucking took Sephie," I snarl as soon as he answers.

"Fuck! I'm coming down right now," He tells me and I hear Mia in the background.

"No, your girl just had a baby. You need to stay there," I tell him. By this time I'm opening my car door and getting in.

"I'm going with you," Silas says.

"Mia needs you. She's probably freaking out right now," I tell him, staring the engine.

"You're right," He admits. "I'll call Ace and he'll meet you wherever you're at."

"I have to find Sephie now. Tell Ace to meet me at the MC's meet up," I hang up before he can say anything else, pulling out of the parking lot.

I follow the nurse's direction, the whole time hoping I'll get there fast enough to save Sephie.

I speed past traffic, a couple of cars blowing their horns at me. I ignore them, intent on finding Sephie and bringing her home to me safely. The MC's meet up is on the other side of town but I get there in fifteen minutes. Like the gym, It's an abandoned warehouse but this one isn't well maintained. Weeds are growing around it and the building is almost falling apart.

I'm out of the car as soon as it stops, stomping over to the door and ripping it open. A couple of dozen mc members are here, lingering around the room. All eyes are on me.

"Where the fuck is Sephie?" I growl at them.

"Can't tell you that. You pay up the fifty grand and we'll tell you," One of the mc members tell me.

"I'll pay up when I have proof that Sephie is unharmed," I tell them. Fifty grand is nothing, not after the money I got from my last fight. I don't care if they want a million dollars, I'll pay anything to get Sephie home. After I get her though, there will be hell to pay. No one harms what's mine and gets to live to tell the story.

"Fine," He says. He pulls out his phone and presses a few buttons before showing me the image on the screen. It's sephie, lying on a ratty couch unconscious, her legs and arms tied up. Fury boils under my skin seeing her like that.

"Give me the address," I say coldly.

"We need the funds," He answers back.

"I'll call my bank and have it transferred to you in ten minutes. I need an address first."

"You know I can't do that."

"Give the address and I just might let you live after this," I tell him. He looks angry at my threat but I think he knows the connections I have because he tells me the address that's in the town over.

Ace is outside when I leave the building, having transferred fifty grand to Moses's account.

"Let's roll," I tell him, getting into my car. He nods, following me in. The only thought in my head is getting Sephie back home safely.

***

Sephie's POV

I wake up with a strong pounding in my head. I pry my eyes open and try to get up and survey my surroundings. I'm on a couch, in what looks like very worn-down house. Confused, I try to think of how I got here. I get flashes of memories, a menacing voice, cold steel pressed against my head, the barrel of a gun slamming into my temple. The realization hits me of what happened. I spot the front door and try to run towards it while I have the chance. I end up falling to the floor, my wrist and ankles bound by zip ties.

"So she still has a little fight in her," An amused cold voice says from above me. This person is different than the man who kidnapped me. He has dark brown hair and cold blue eyes that stare down at me in cold humor. He just as tall and big as Dominic and I know there is no way I can out un run him. I unsuccessfully try to scramble away from him with my bound feet and hands.

"I'm not going to hurt you. You're much too valuable, a lot of money can be made off of you," He calmly walks toward me and grabs me by the arm, sitting me back on the couch next to him.

"Why are you doing this to me! My mother is the one who owes you money so why don't you just kidnap her!" I scream in frustration, tears running down my face. My whole life I've had to pay for her mistakes and although I wouldn't wish this on anyone, I'm tired of taking the fall for her.

"That would be hard, considering she's dead," My body tenses in surprise.

"When we got to her she was dead in her hotel room. Overdosed on cocaine after burning through my money. Only five thousand dollars was left of it. You can imagine I'm not too happy about being played out of fifty grand."

"This still has nothing to do with me. You should have been more careful with your money," I regret my words immediately when his face gets dark.

"This has everything to do with you. It would have been you're sister we were after since she's your mother's first child but she got lucky, being with Silas. You were such an easy target, so vulnerable with no one to protect you. Then your little boyfriend messed that up. Now he's got a choice, give me the fifty thousand or let his innocent little girlfriend work for it with her body."

"You're a monster," I spit out at him in anger.

"I'm very aware of that, sweet Sephie. You've got bad luck, getting caught up with the likes of me. Just hope I don't let Samuel defile you before sending you home to your boyfriend. He's not too happy with you after that stunt you pulled and he wouldn't be very gentle with you."

With that, he lives me on the couch, a mixture of fear and anger brewing in me. I pray that Dominic gets to me in time.

***

I sit on the worn couch, body aching and stomach-turning. I worry about Dominic and Mia. I can't imagine how worried they are right now. This supposed to be a happy day for Mia and she has to worry about her sister being kidnapped. I can't help but feel guilty at the pain I'm putting on everyone around me.

Samuel makes another appearance about an hour after the other man left. His eyes come to me as soon as he's in the room, narrowed in little slits.

"You're lucky her little boyfriend paid up," Samuel says to him, glaring eyes still on me. I don't feel relief that the debt is paid, just guilt that Dominic had to go through all this trouble because of my problems

"I think you owe me after all the trouble you put me through,"

I cower far away from him on the couch. I'm still tied up so there isn't much I can do to defend myself.

"Dominic's coming for me. He'll be here any minute," I warn him, earning a cold smirk.

"Then I should make the most of our time together."

I push myself off the couch and onto the floor, trying to get away from him with my hands and legs bound as he makes his way towards. I'm not nearly fast enough and he pulls me by the arm and throws me back on the couch. All over again, It's the scene from the trailer all those months ago except now I can't fight back. I thrash under him, trying to buck him off to no avail. He puts his hand over my mouth to cover my screaming. Just like the day at the trailer, I bite it as hard as I can.

"Fuckin bitch!" He pulls back and slams his fist into my stomach. I cry out at the sharp pain in my lower stomach. Through the pain I still try to fight him off as he tries to get my top off of me. In the back of my mind I know there's no point in fighting anymore and he's eventually going to overpower me.

My thrashing slows down once my top is completely off and I'm close to giving up. He tries to get my bra and suddenly his weight completely off of me. I scurry off of the couch, in the back of my head noticing how the sharp pain in my lower stomach is getting more intense. I pull my hoodie back on, grimacing through the pain.

A few feet away I notice the commotion that got Samuel off of me. I'm filled with relief that Dominic is here but that's quickly overshadowed by fear. He is viciously beating Samuel and I wince at the sounds of his fist hitting Samuel's flesh. Dominic looks furious, completely intent on causing as much pain as possible. I know if I don't stop him he's going to kill him.

"Dominic...you have to stop," I tell him in a pleading voice. His eyes come to me and he immediately leaves Samuel a bloody mess on the floor to rush over to me, Pulling me in his arms.

"Sephie, I'm so sorry I let this happen," He tells me sorrowfully.

"It's not your fault," I tell him. I want to tell him more but the pain in my lower stomach is now agonizing, making it hard to stay standing. Black dots are clouding my vision and I groan, clutching my stomach at the pain.

"Sephie, are you alright?" Dominic says, panicking.

"I think I need a doctor," I tell him. That's the last thing I say before the whole world tilts and goes black.

Sorry that I didn't update yesterday, I just needed a little break.

I hope you guys liked this chapter. If you did, leave a vote!

Chapter Thirty

Dominic's POVAce and I arrive at a small run-down house in a bad neighborhood. I check the address and this is it. Sephie's inside of here, injured and hurting. I hop out of the car as soon as its at a full stop. A man is standing outside. I recognize the cold eyes and dark brown hair - it's Moses. As soon as I see him I want to kill him. This is the man behind all of Sephie's suffering the past months."Where the fuck is Sephie," I ask, holding myself back."She's right inside. Pleasure doing business with you," He says with a sly smirk. I know he has something up his sleeve and I waste no time rushing past him into the rugged house.Inside there is a struggle going on on the couch. I see a man's figure on top of a girl, who is thrashing beneath him and looks as if her hands are tied behind her back. I notice her brown curls and recognize her as Sephie. My Sephie. My vision goes red as I charge the man, pulling him off of her. I still see red as I slam my fist into his face over and over, feeling the distinct crack of his nose under my fist."Dominic...you have to stop," I hear Sephies scared voice and leave the man lying there. All that matters right now is her."Sephie, I'm so sorry I let this happen," I tell her after taking her into my arms. I should have never let her leave that hospital room alone knowing the dangers out there."It's not your fault," She tells me softly. Suddenly, she clutches her stomach, groaning in pain."Sephie, are you alright?" I ask, panicking. I've never seen Sephie in this much pain before and It's almost unbearable to witness."I think I need a doctor," Sephie says, her voice a faint whisper. Then I see her eyes close and she falls over, nearly hitting the floor if I didn't catch her."Shit," I growl, picking her up. I need to get her to the hospital immediately. When I get outside, Ace is already starting the car again. I put her in the backseat. When I close the car door behind her, I notice Moses's figure, Still standing by the door."You're going to pay for this," I promise. He has no reaction other than putting on his cold smirk. I'll handle him later, Sephie needs me.I get in the backseat with Sephie, her head resting on my lap. As I push her hair back from her temple I see swelling and dark bruising on her temple. My teeth grit together. I'm going to make them all pay for this.Ace speeds to the hospital and we arrive there in no time. I hurry out of the car and pick up Sephie, cradling her in my arms. A doctor rushes over as soon as he sees me carrying her in. Sephie is put on a stretcher, still not regaining consciousness. I try to go in with her but I'm stopped by a nurse."You can't go in there," He tells me."I need to be in there for her!" I spit out. His face pales a bit at my anger."Y-Your just going to have to wait until we treat her, sir. We'll give you an update when we find the problem," Reluctantly, I agree to stay out of the room. I decide to update Mia and Silas on what happened.When I get into the room, Mia jumps up immediately, but Silas forces her to sit down, not wanting her to exert herself after giving birth."Is she okay?" She asks worriedly."I got her back but not unharmed. It looked like she had a pain in her stomach before she fainted. I also noticed a bruise on her temple. The nurse says he hit her with his gun," I say the last part through grit teeth, imaging him hurting my Sephie."I'm going to kill him," The usually nice-looking Mia growls out through grit teeth. Luckily Mila is sleeping in her little bed, oblivious to all of this."My thoughts exactly," I agree."We can't let them get away with," Silas says and I have to agree."Let the police handle it. I don't want you getting in trouble," Mia says"I'll let Sephie press charges but that doesn't mean I'm not going to kick Samuel's ass," I tell them. "As for Moses, we need to handle him. The cops have been after him for years, to no avail. I'll let him be an example of what happens when you mess with the people I care about."As we wait for an update on Sephie, there is a tense silence. I know Mia doesn't want us to do anything illegal but she knows she can't talk us out of it. It isn't until an hour later that a doctor comes in to give an update on Sephie."Is she going to be okay?" I ask, sitting up in my seat, alert."Yes, Mr. Hayes. She has a minor concussion from her head injury and will need to rest for the next week," I sink in my seat in relief, happy that she's okay."I'm not sure if you were aware of this, Mr. Hayes, but Sephie was carrying. She has miscarried due to trauma to her lower abdomen.""What?" I ask in complete shock. I feel like my whole world has been turned upside down. Sephie was pregnant with my baby? I have a vision of her in my head, stomach swollen with my child, cradling a little bundle in her arms. I feel the sharp sting of loss at what could have been."I'm sorry for your loss, Mr. Hayes. I send my condolences," The doctor says before leaving us."I'm so sorry, Dominic," Mia says softly. Silas offers a comforting hand on my shoulder. None of this lifts my heavy heart, though, as I think about breaking this news to Sephie when she wakes up.

Chapter Thirty-One

- -

S ephie's POV.I wake up with a throbbing head and dry mouth. I try to pry my eyes open but the bright white lights force them close. I do this a couple of times before my eyes adjust. I'm laying in a hospital bed in a hospital gown. I lift my hand to see where the throbbing in my temple is coming from but the IV connected to my arm stops me."Sephie? You're awake!" Dominic's voice comforts me and I calm down. He brings his chair to my bedside and sits next to me, hand intertwining with mine."I'm fine. Just a little thirsty," Dominic jumps up immediately at my words, filling a styrofoam cup with the water pitcher and coming back to hand it to me.I sit up in the bed and sip at the cold water, welcoming the cold drink in my parched throat. I down it in a few gulps and Dominic takes it and feels it up for me again."Do you have any pain? Do I need to get the nurse to give you some more pain medicine?" Dominic asks after he hands me the cup."No, I'm alright," I tell him, even though my head is throbbing. I shift in the bed and a sharp pain shoots from my lower stomach, making me wince. Without question, Dominic buzzes for a nurse. She comes in moments later and Dominic tells her I need more medicine. She gives me two white pills, which I happily take with my water, wanting the throbbing in my head to stop."What happened?" I ask Dominic once the nurse leaves. " I remember being kidnapped outside the hospital...and some man attacking me on a couch. After that it gets fuzzy.""A man was attacking you when I got there. I got him off of you and when I asked if you were okay you fainted," Dominic's face gets grim as he says the next part. "The Doctor said you have a minor concussion. He also said that you were...pregnant. I'm sorry Sephie, but you had a miscarriage."I'm stock still as I absorb this information. I was pregnant with Dominic's child. The thought of a little Dominic growing inside me sends a fleeting feeling of joy in me followed by sorrow. I lost the baby. The baby I didn't even know I had."Samuel...he hit me in the stomach. I should've fought harder. If I had just gotten him off of me-""None of this is your fault," Dominic says cutting me off. "This is their fault. There was nothing you could have done to stop this, Sephie.""I can't believe I was pregnant," I tell him. And then I burst into tears, not just at this loss but everything I've been through these past few months. Dominic pulls me into his arms, at an awkward angle because of the IV in my arm."One day we'll try again, Sephie. I promise," Dominic words calm me and the sobs die down."Are we interrupting something?" Mia's voice comes from the door. She and Silas are standing at the door awkwardly."No! Come in," I say hurriedly, wiping the tears from my cheeks. Mia comes over and stands by my side at the bed."I'm so sorry, Sephie. After having Mila I can't even imagine what you're going through right now," Mia says, squeezing my hand."Thank you for being here. How's the baby?" I ask her and her face lights up."She sleeps all day. I've only gotten to see her eyes open a handful of times and she has Silas's eyes."Mia tells me all about her baby and how the nursery back home is going. I welcome the distraction from my own problems, but soon I feel my eyelids getting heavy."The pain medicine must be kicking in. I'll leave you be and let you rest," Mia leans down and places a kiss on my cheek before leaving with Silas.Dominic's hand intertwines with mine again as I let the drowsiness take over. My eyes drift closed and Dominic stays by my side as I fall asleep.***When I wake up Dominic is gone and I'm alone in the hospital room. There is a note by my bedside by Dominic, saying he went out to handle some business. My head is throbbing again and the ache in my lower abdomen reminds me of my miscarriage. I call in a nurse for more pain medicine, happily gulping down those white pills. When the nurse leaves, Mia comes in with her baby."I heard you were awake and thought a visit from your niece would cheer you up," Mia says, placing the little bundle in my arms. Mila is awake now, looking up at me with her wide greyish blue eyes. Mia was right, she doesn't have the light brown ones passed onto us by our mom. I coo at the little baby and like all newborns, she just stares up in awe at the new face."I can't believe I'm an aunt," I tell her, looking up from Mila's adorable face."I still can't believe I'm a mom," Mia says, sitting in the chair next to my bed. "I'm really scared. You know how our mom is so we both know what having a bad mom is like. I don't want Mila to go through that.""You are nothing like our mom!" I tell her, sitting up in my bed. "You're going to be a wonderful mom and Mila is going to be lucky to have you in her life.""Speaking of our mom," Sephie says, looking apprehensive. "You probably already know she passed away. Her side of the family holding a funeral for her a week from now. You don't have to go if you don't want to.""I don't know. I still haven't come to terms with this. How do you grieve someone who hurt you so much?" I tell her. Most of my life I had to deal with her neglect and alcohol abuse. I feel a sting of guilt that I'm not sad at her death."Like I said, you don't have to come. I don't know if I'm going either," Mia admits to me.Mila falls asleep again so Mia takes her back up to her hospital room and I'm alone again. Being cramped up in the hospital room is making me claustrophobic and I want to go home. I'm anxiously tapping my fingers against the rail of the hospital bed when Dominic comes in. My face lights up at his presence but then he gets closer and I notice the split lip he's sporting."Dominic! What happened?" I ask him, brows furrowed with worry."I had to take care of something," He says, not elaborating further."Did you..." I trail off, knowing the answer."You won't have to worry about them again," Dominic promises fiercely."You didn't have to do that, Dominic! You could've gotten hurt or worse!""I'm fine, Sephie. What's done is done and nothing like this will ever happen again. If you want to press charges on them, go ahead, but either way, you won't be hearing from them ever again.""Dominic..." I whisper, not knowing how to feel about this. "I don't want you to put yourself in harm's way over me.""I know and I'll do it anyway. You have to know, Sephie, that's what you're going to get with me. I'm not the kind of man to sit back and let his woman get hurt," I'm silent for a second, absorbing his words. There is little flurry going on in my stomach at Dominic calling me 'his woman'. At the same time I know he's right. In the back of my head, I always knew that Dominic wouldn't let them get away with this."Okay," I give in finally. "I won't be pressing charges. I trust that you...handled things."At my words, Dominic leans down and places a kiss on my forehead."My sephie," He whispers, breath fanning over my face.

Chapter Thirty-Two

A /N: Sorry that this chapter is so short, this scene couldn't really fit in with the chapters before it or after it.

Dominic's POVI leave the abandoned building with Ace, my fist bloodied and lip busted. Samuel and Moses won't be a problem for Sephie ever again. From the example I just set, no one else will be either.I drop Ace off before going back home. I want to go back to the hospital to be with Sephie, but Rocky needs to be fed and I have an important phone call to make. As soon as I come into the house, Rocky is at the door, rubbing his little head against my legs. Poor guy has been here by himself all day. I open a can of cat food and put it in his bowl, giving his soft head a quick scratch. Then I pick up my phone and dial the number I have known since childhood."Dominic! How are you doing, honey?" My mother's voice answers sweetly."Not good," I admit. "Sephies's in the hospital. She was at tacked.""Oh no, poor Sephie! I'm so sorry, dear," Mom says sympathetica lly."She's healing very fast but that's not why I called.""What is it then," She asks."Mom, is there any way I can get grandma's old wedding ring?""Oh my god! Are you proposing!?" She squeals like a little girl."Yeah, Mom. Sephie the one, I know it. She's my forever," I tell her. I've been thinking about this for a while now. I want to spend my life with Sephie. When we were in that hospital room after I broke the news of the miscarriage and I told her that we can try again one day, I meant it. I want Sephie to be the one I spend my life with and I want her to be the one who has my children."I'm so happy for you guys. My little boy has finally found happiness," Mom says, sniffling. "I still have your grandmother's ring. I'll have it over to you as soon as possible.""Thank you, Mom. I love you," I tell her."I love you too. Tell Sephie I said hello."With that, I disconnect and go back out to see Sephie at the hospital.

Chapter Thirty-Three

Two weeks later

I twist around to fully appraise myself in the mirror. The flowy skirt twirls with my movements. It took a lot for me to build the confidence to wear the peach-colored dress, the top hugging my curves in a revealing way. Luckily, Dee and Mia were there when I bought it, boosting my confidence.The city fair is coming back to town for a week during the summer. I almost leaped out of my skin with joy when Dominic told me he was taking me on a date there. Now, I grab my purse from our bed. Our bed. It sounds strange to say it. There was some confusion when I got back from the hospital, me thinking I would go home to the trailer now that the threat was gone. Dominic nearly had a stroke when he saw me packing my duffle bag. He quickly explained to me that this stopped being about me needing his protection a long time ago.

Once the bag is secured around my shoulder, I nearly skip out to meet Dominic by the car. I jump into his arms, something that I wouldn't have been able to do two weeks ago when I was still recovering from the attack."I'm so excited!" I nearly squeal, thinking about all the cotton candy and rides."I can see," Dominic chuckles, setting me down and opening the door for me to get in the car. The whole way there I talk about all the rides and foods I heard will be at the fair. Dominic lets me gush, chuckling when I get really excited about something. When we get to the fairgrounds I excitedly wait for Dominic to come around and open my door. I get out and he leads me inside, hand on the small of my back."What should we do first? The go-carts or Ferris wheel," I ask him, the smell of popcorn and cotton candy making my stomach growl."Let's save the Ferris wheel for last. And from the sound of it, the first thing we need is snacks," I blush at the fact that he heard my ravenous stomach. Dominic buys us both a corn dog and slushy and we look around at all of the rides and games as we finish our snacks.Dominic and I have a blast, riding the go-carts, and seeing everything the fair has to offer. By the time we reach the Ferris wheel, we have been to every other attraction at the fair and it's early evening, the sky just starting to turn shades of pink and orange.Dominic helps me into our carriage, getting in behind me, and I watch in amazement as we lift off of the ground, the view absolutely stunning."Isn't it beautiful?" I say to Dominic, looking at the gorgeous view of our city."It is," Dominic says, sounding just as star-struck as me. When I turn around to give him a smile, his eyes aren't on the view at all, but on me."Dominic?" I question, brow furrowing."Sephie," He begins. "I have never met someone with a heart as pure as yours. Your beauty, your kindness...it captured me from the moment I first laid eyes on you. I was amazed that you couldn't see it, the way you draw in everyone around you with your kind soul. I still mean every word I said to you on the night of our last time at the carnival. Not only am I going to make you see your beauty but I want to spend my whole life doing it.""Dominic," I whisper voice thick with tears of joy. I stare in amazed happiness as he pulls out a small black velvet box."Sephie Mckay, I love you more than words can express. Will you be my wife?"I stare at the beautiful ring, glimmering with the lights of the fair. My mind goes back to every moment leading up to this, me first laying eyes on him, that night after the carnival, tracing every inch of his body with my fingertips, crying into his chest at the hospital, him holding my hand at my mother's funeral only a week ago. If I could back I would thank her, because without her I would have never met Dominic. Looking into his eyes, I know in my heart that he's the love of my life. So I give him the only answer there is."Yes."

Chapter Thirty-Four

A/N: This chapter is NSFW, read at your own discretion.

Mia stares at the ring on my finger, the beautiful silver band adorned with shimmering white diamonds.

"Oh my god! He put a ring on it!" Mia screams, alerting everyone in the bookshop. Dee just gives me a cheerful look, her knowing about Dominic's plans to propose to me weeks before it happened.

"What is this I hear about a ring," Leah says, coming over to the table. She gasps when she sees the rock on my finger.

"Congrats, girlie!" She says, bending down to give me a side hug.

"Thank you. I've already started planning things for the wedding. It's going to be small, twenty guests at top, and I want it to be at the beach," I tell them, glowing with joy. I never thought I would be planning my dream wedding, not in a million years.

"I'm really happy for you, Sephie. Dominic brings out the best in you," This comes from Chris, who has walked over to the coffee nook.

"Thank you, Chris. I really appreciate that," I tell him. Since I got back from the hospital, things have not been awkward between us and that night at the carnival has been left in the past, where it belongs.

"How's the nursery going?" I ask Mia after Chris leaves.

"It's done and it looks amazing. Since Dominic started helping Silas out with the business he was able to help," I smile at that. Since Dominic is done with fighting, something I was surprised and relieved to hear, he and Silas have been working together and it looks like he's going to become his business partner.

For the rest of my time there, Mia and Dee and help me brainstorm ideas for the wedding and a few of the customers come over to congratulate me. Before I leave, Leah gives me a box of sugar cookies in celebration of my engagement.

It's strange, driving by myself home. Since I'm no longer in danger I don't need someone with me 24/7. Still, Dominic and I are together most of the day.

I set the cookies on the counter when I get home, taking my shoes off on the way to our bedroom. I jump when I open the door to Dominic, shirtless on the bed.

"I didn't know you in here," I say giving a nervous chuckle.

"How'd it go?" Dominic asks.

"Mia freaked out, Dee was calm, because she knew your whole scheme. I can't believe she kept a straight face for two whole weeks, the little fibber."

"You think you had it bad? She was bustin' my balls the whole time," Dominic says with a chuckle.

"Now, come over here, Mrs. Hayes," Dominic says with a devilish smirk. The butterflies who have made a home in my stomach since I first laid eyes on Dominic make themselves known at his new name for me. Even though we're not married yet, Dominic has taken to calling me that and it never gets old.

I crawl onto the bed on all fours, matching his smirk as I make my way over to him. Since being with Dominic I have gained so much confidence. Months ago I would have been too shy to do this but now I know in my heart that Dominic loves everything about me, as I do him.

I crawl onto his lap and my mouth meets his for a heated kiss. My hands tangle into his hair, loving the feel of the silky strands. Dominic's hands settle themselves on my hips as he takes my lips roughly. I moan into his mouth, heat filling my core. As the kiss gets more sensual I start to grind my hips on his and I gasp at the pleasurable feeling that comes with it.

"Fuck, Sephie," Dominic growls against my lips. He pushes me and I land on my back, and he's kneeling over be, lips leaving hot trails of kisses down my throat. He licks an extra sensitive area there and I cry out, desperate for him. My hand pulls his shirt up and he separates for just a second to pull it off. Then he's back again, mouth on mine, unbuttoning my blouse. I lift up a bit to take it off, lips still on his. He's trailing down again reaching behind me to take off my bra.

My back arches when he takes my nipple into his mouth. His other hand comes up to twist the other one and I cry out. I reach down and unbutton my jeans, needing him to take me. he pulls them off for me and I miss his mouth on my breast but only for a second because moments later his mouth is on my core making me scream.

My fingers find their way into his hair and I'm glad we don't have any neighbors close by because they would definitely hear my screams of pleasure. Dominic works me over, to the brink of climax and back down again.

I'm frustrated almost to the point of tears, wanting release badly Then his mouth is gone and I feel frustration building.

"Dominic, please!" I plead desperately.

"Patience," He says, pulling the belt out of his jeans and unbuttoning them. When he's just as naked as me, he's back between my thighs, my sensitive breast rubbing against his chest. His lips are on mine again as he positions his self against. My nails dig into his back at his first thrust, face a mask of silent pleasure. He doesn't give me time to adjust like he usually does, just pounds into me until I'm screaming his name. The pleasure is so intense that I bite down on his shoulder just to keep the screams at bay.

"Fuck, Dominic, just like that" I cry out. An animalistic groan leaves Dominic and his thrusts get faster. I know it drives him crazy when I talk dirty so I've made mental a note to do it often when we make love.

Dominic's hand reaches between us and he rubs my clit as he thrust. This sets me off and I'm coming around him, screaming his name as my fingers claw at his back. I come down from my high and Dominic's thrusts get uneven as he finds his climax.

Afterward, we lay in bed, my head on his chest, basking in the afterglow of our love-making.

"I'll never get enough of this," Dominic whispers, breath fanning over the top of my head. I can't help thinking that I'll never get enough of this either.

Chapter Thirty-Five

I stare at myself in the floor-length mirror, admiring the beauty of the white dress. The sweetheart neckline hugs me in the most flattering way, the delicate white lace detailing and Swarovski crystals simply stunning. The dress hugs me all the way down to my hips, where it flares out, the crystals getting sparse, only a faint glimmer until they disappear at the knee.

I wanted to straighten my hair but Mia had other ideas, twisting a few strands and arranging my curls in an elegant bun at the back of my head. Dee did my makeup, a natural look with a soft rose blush and a lipstick to match. I couldn't even recognize the girl in the mirror, she was radiant and beautiful all at once. Or better yet, she was here all along, I just couldn't see her. Dominic's words from all those nights ago repeat themselves in my head, ringing truer over time. I am beautiful, I tell myself. This time, I believe it.

"You look gorgeous," Mia says, coming behind me and wrapping her arms around me in a tight hug.

"I know," I tell her, admiring myself.

"I've been trying to get you to see that for years," Mia says with a playful eye roll.

"We've found it," She says, voice suddenly thick with emotion.

"What?" I ask, brow creasing with worry.

"Happiness. We used to talk about this when we were little girls, how we'd meet the loves of our lives and get married and have kids. We finally got it, after everything we've been through."

"It's like a fairytale come true," I whisper, my voice thick with emotion too now.

"What did I tell you about making the bride cry," Judy's shrill voice makes us jump, ending the sentimental moment.

"You're lucky you have on water proof mascara, Dee would have a stroke if she had to redo your makeup."

"Judy! You nearly gave us a stroke," Mia says.

"Look at my future daughter in law," Judy cries out when she sees the dress.

"Simply stunning. I couldn't have asked for a better woman for my son," She tells me, hands on my shoulder while appraising me.

"Thank you. You have no idea how much that means to me," I tell her, trying to keep tears at bay.

"I trust you'll take good care of my boy," She says, looking like she's going to cry now.

"You have my word."

"Then get your behind out there. He's waiting."

"Oh my god, it's time already!" I say, freaking out.

"It is. Don't fret, my love. You'll be perfect out there," Judy says, before kissing both of my cheeks. Mia gives me a hug before leaving to take her place as my bridesmaid.

I'm left alone in the little room. I go stand by the door and I can hear the music the bridesmaid and best man walk out to. When the song changes it will be my cue to walk down the isle. I take a couple of deep breaths, rehearsing my vows.

The music changes and I follow my cue. I can do this, I tell myself. I step out of the room into the outdoors, Lifting my dress so it won't drag on the sand. A couple of white chairs are set out, an isle between them. All of our close friends and family are here, giving me encouraging looks. Across from me stands Dominic, so handsome in his black suit that I forget how to breathe for a second. Next to him is Silas, in a blue suit and on his other side is Mia, in a blue dress, holding her six-month-old baby girl who is in a light blue frilly dress. In the background of all of them, the blue ocean waves crash onto the shore.

I walk to the beat of the soft music played by the violinist, my eyes on Dominic's the whole time. I feel no fear now, knowing that everything is going to be alright just from looking into his eyes.

I finally reach Dominic and I'm standing across from him, my hands in his big strong ones.

We repeat after the minister, the whole time we look into each other's eyes, tears of happiness flooding mine. When it's our turn to say our vows, Dominic goes first.

"Sephie, no man has known the happiness I feel in this moment, standing in front of you. You complete me, in a way no other person on this earth can. The day when I first laid eyes on you I knew that fate was shining down on us. I will spend every day of my life showing you how thankful I am that you let me into your heart. You are my destiny, Sephie." Tears are flowing down my cheeks when he's done, pure joy shining through me. I start my vows before I get too choked up to speak.

"Dominic, before I met you I was lost. You didn't necessarily find me, but you help me find myself and for that, I am forever thankful. You helped me see the beauty in myself and in the world. I look forward to spending the rest of my life with you. You captured my heart and it's forever yours now."

Tears glimmer on my cheeks as the minister tells Dominic to kiss his bride. He leans down and his lips brush over mine softly.

"Forever," He whispers.

"Forever," I promise.

www.ingramcontent.com/pod-product-compliance
Lightning Source LLC
Chambersburg PA
CBHW070401200726
48294CB00003B/1027